TROUBLE
IN DEEP LAKE

TROUBLE IN DEEP LAKE

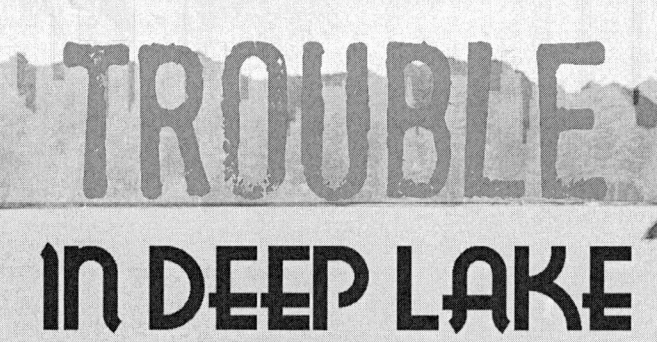

GLORIA VAN

Trouble In Deep Lake © Copyright 2021 by Gloria VanDemmeltraadt

All rights reserved. No part of this book may be reproduced in any form or by any means, electronic or mechanical, including photocopying, recording, or by any information storage and retrieval system, without written permission from the author.

This is a work of fiction. Names, characters, places, and incidents either are products of the author's imagination or are used fictitiously. Any resemblance to actual events or locales or persons, living or dead, is entirely coincidental.

First Edition

ISBN: 9781952976155
LOC: 2021904499

First Printing March, 2021

Cover design and interior design by Kirk House Publishers
Back cover photo used with permission by photographer Jessi Shepherd, owner of Golden Retriever Barkalona (aka Lona), and assisted by Diane Morgan.
Map of Deep Lake by Roxanne Rosell and author

Kirk House Publishers
1250 E 115th Street
Burnsville, MN 55337
612-781-2815

ACKNOWLEDGMENTS

As every author knows, no book is written by one person alone. It's a scary, exciting, rewarding, and humiliating adventure with many advisers, supporters, critique-givers, and more who are dragged along for the ride.

This story, along with the other Deep Lake adventures, is totally a figment of my imagination. Deep Lake is a fictional town made up of elements of a number of Minnesota communities. Fond du Lac and Oshkosh are real places in Wisconsin, with a few real historical details tossed in, but all the rest is fiction. I hope their residents enjoy the story.

I give sincere thanks to my fellow writers in the WOW (Women of Words) writing group. The information and expertise we share is priceless.

Thank you in particular to M.J. Schultz, Susan Schussler, and Cathy Cowen for encouragement and endless support. Thanks, too, to Connie Anderson, Charlene Roemhildt, Ann Wieland, Roxanne Rosell, and Paul Cannon for technical help, plus Toni, Miki, Diane, Gisela and Judy for lending their hands and feet.

Above all, thank you to my family; children, steps, grandchildren, and greats all for caring so much, and my patient loving husband, Onno, for laughing, listening, and pouring the wine.

Gloria

MAP OF DEEP LAKE

(not drawn to scale)

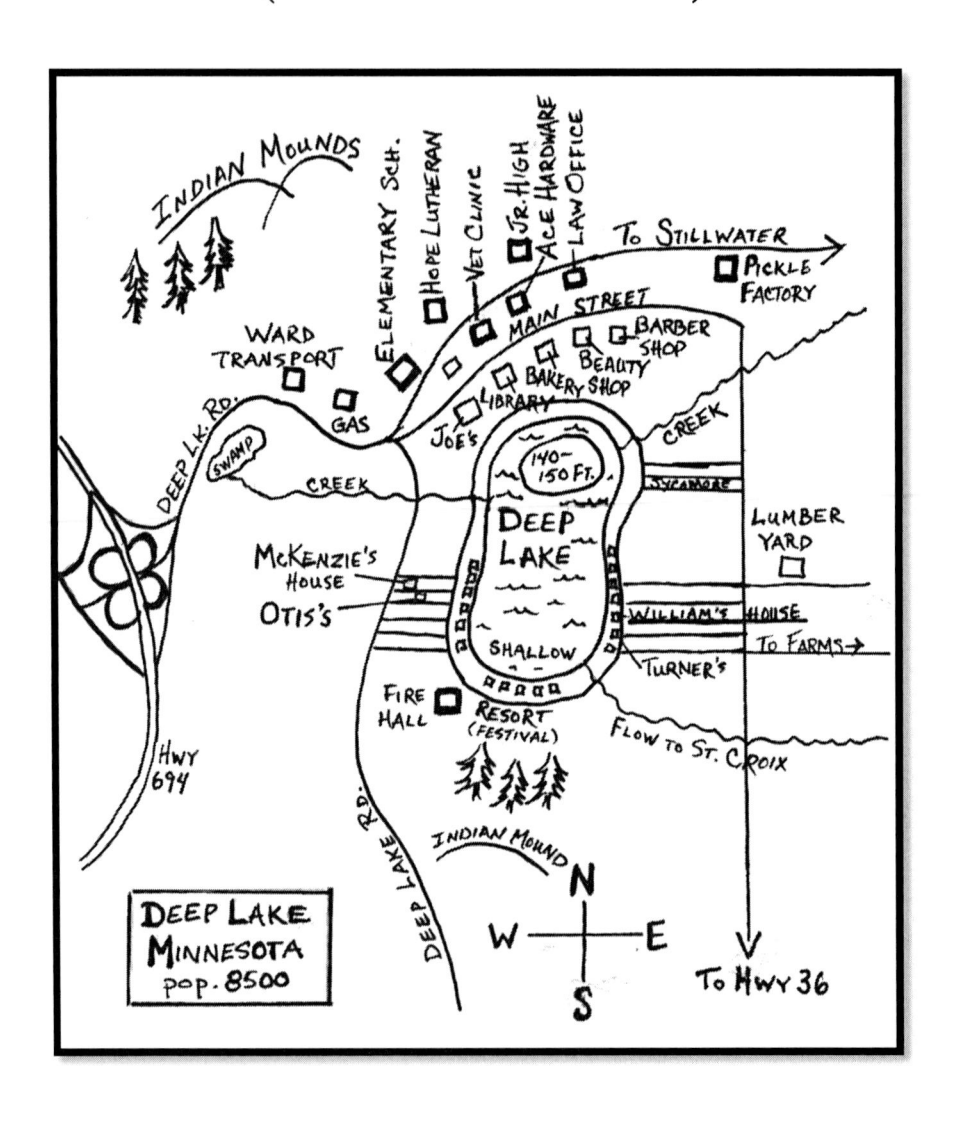

TABLE OF CONTENTS

Cast of Characters 9
Chapter 1 Problem in NYC 11
Chapter 2 Arriving Back in New York City 19
Chapter 3 Darkness in Deep Lake 23
Chapter 4 The First Day Back in NYC 27
Chapter 5 Deep Lake Without McKenzie 37
Chapter 6 Reconnecting with NYC 41
Chapter 7 Trouble in Deep Lake 47
Chapter 8 Unwanted Advanced in NYC 51
Chapter 9 Clinic Destroyed in Deep Lake 55
Chapter 10 Investigations in NYC 59
Chapter 11 A Surprising Arrest in Deep Lake 67
Chapter 12 Agony in Deep Lake 71
Chapter 13 NYC Good News and Bad News 75
Chapter 14 Bad News from Deep Lake 81
Chapter 15 Janice Goes to NYC 85
Chapter 16 Arraignment in Deep Lake 89
Chapter 17 Friends Connect in NYC 93
Chapter 18 Ethan Suffers in Deep Lake 97
Chapter 19 Questionable Massage in NYC 101
Chapter 20 Interviewing in Deep Lake 105
Chapter 21 Discovery in NYC 109
Chapter 22 Interviews Continue in Deep Lake 113
Chapter 23 Shock in NYC 117

Chapter 24 The Plot Thickens in NYC 121

Chapter 25 More Questions in NYC 125

Chapter 26 Surprising Arrests in NYC 129

Chapter 27 More Discussions in NYC 135

Chapter 28 Cleaning up in NYC................................. 143

Chapter 29 Back to Deep Lake 149

Chapter 30 At Home in Deep Lake 155

Chapter 31 Issues in Fond du Lac............................... 163

Chapter 32 Questions in Fond du Lac 169

Chapter 33 Return to Deep Lake 187

Chapter 34 Trouble Compounded in Deep Lake 197

Chapter 35 Kidnapped in Deep Lake 203

Chapter 36 Somewhere in Wisconsin 209

Chapter 37 Breakthrough in Deep Lake..................... 213

Chapter 38 Anxiety in Deep Lake 219

Chapter 39 Shock in Oshkosh 223

Chapter 40 Trouble Resolved in Deep Lake............... 227

About the Author 233

CAST OF CHARACTERS

McKenzie (Kenzie) Ward, beautiful and successful commercial real estate exec from New York came back to Deep Lake, her hometown in Minnesota, when her father died. Now a local Realtor, and amateur sleuth.

Otis Jorgensen, Assistant Sheriff of Washington County and McKenzie's childhood best friend. His wife is **Mary Jo** (Hanson), and sons are **Albert** and **Ben**, nine and eight years old.

Ethan Thompson, Deep Lake veterinarian, widower, considered hot and eligible, McKenzie's current boyfriend.

Isabella Thompson, six-year-old daughter of Ethan and her deceased mother, **Elizabeth**. Isabella's grandmother is **Grandma Jane Rostad**, Elizabeth's mother.

Michael Romano, McKenzie's former boyfriend in New York City (NYC), handsome and successful lawyer.

Desirée Canard, Commercial Realtor—partner of McKenzie in her office in the Ward Building in NYC. Beautiful French bombshell.

Gayle Granville, McKenzie and Desirée's secretary and office manager in NYC.

Joyce and Luke Thompson, Ethan's parents; **Bethany and Aaron Gifford**, Ethan's sister and husband, have three small children. All live in Wisconsin.

James Archer Ward, McKenzie's father, and a former Minnesota judge, died in 2017 of wasp stings. **Rose Anne Weber Ward**, McKenzie's mother, died in 2001.

William James Ward, McKenzie's older brother, works at Ward Transport, owned by the family. His wife, **Dolly**, died in 2018. His daughter, **Sophia**, is currently in college.

Ed Johnson, long-time manager of Ward Transport, started by **Big Jim Ward**, McKenzie's grandfather who died in 1983.

Janice Hopkins, good friend of McKenzie's since high school, owns beauty shop in Deep Lake.

Vicky (Vidal) Vargas, Brazilian exchange student who returned to Deep Lake after a gender change. Works with Janice and is friends with McKenzie.

Tracey Freeman, friend of McKenzie's from work. Lives in Woodbury with husband **Oliver**, and has twins, boy and girl, age four.

Howard, Fred, and George, old guys who sit in front of Ace Hardware and McKenzie's coffee buddies at Joe's restaurant.

Sheriff Gary Walker, Sheriff of Washington County.

Lieutenant Lloyd Strother, Otis's deputy in the Deep Lake office.

CHAPTER 1
PROBLEM IN NYC

McKenzie Ward greeted her caller, "Hey, Desirée, sorry it's been a while, I haven't really been ignoring you, just busy." She leaned down to give her golden retriever, Goldie, a loving pat while sitting at her kitchen counter in Deep Lake, Minnesota, where she had been going over the latest home listings for her real estate business.

Desirée Canard, manager of McKenzie's business interests in New York City, got straight to the point. "We have an issue here that needs your attention."

"What's happening?" McKenzie stood in apprehension.

"There's a problem in your building."

Desirée and McKenzie's friend Gayle had been taking care of her business beautifully since she left Manhattan for her hometown when her father died the previous summer. She had chosen to stay on in her roomy childhood home, and those two women had made her life choice possible.

"A young woman has been found dead in an empty office on second floor."

McKenzie gasped and sat down again.

"The short story is drugs, and I'm afraid you'll have to come to the City to deal with it. The police are insisting because there could be an abduction involved."

"Abduction?! Seriously? How do I fit in?"

"It's early stages, but you own the building and need to be here to deal with things, ASAP. It's messy."

♦♦♦♦♦

With reluctance, McKenzie began to prepare for the New York trip. Life had become comfortable for her back in Deep Lake, after her former successful but frantic years in New York as a Commercial Realtor. She soon came to relish the quiet simplicity of small-town living. She'd fallen in love with her original life all over again, her father's beautiful early 1900s gem of a house, her old friends, and some new ones, too. Especially significant was her blossoming romantic relationship with Ethan Thompson, the town's veterinarian.

The vet clinic was in the heart of downtown Deep Lake, and Ethan cared for animals small and large throughout the community. He even had a sign in front of the clinic that said, "We treat tinted chicks & duckies," in honor of the pink, blue, and green baby chickens and ducks that local children might get for Easter, which was coming soon. Ethan treated McKenzie's dog, Goldie, before she even realized she had inherited the dog from her father. That's how they met the previous summer when her father, who had been fishing buddies with Ethan, was killed.

While packing and making some calls after the upsetting call from Desirée, she thought about how hard it was going to be to leave Ethan, even for a short time. They were quickly and deeply falling in love, and she ached at the thought of being separated from him and his delightful daughter. They often did things as a family, and even though it had been less than a year since they met, the future was looking bright for them to stay with each other. In fact, they were planning to have pizza that night, and McKenzie was looking forward to their special time together after Isabella went to bed.

She knew she must call him immediately. Ginny, the clinic helper, answered, saying he was with a patient but she'd have him return her call shortly.

Thinking back over the past year and all the changes that came about because of the death of Judge James Archer Ward, was dizzying. McKenzie got the family home, and she and her brother, William, together had inherited the family trucking business from their father. William was working with the trucking company and McKenzie had little to do with it.

Her cell jolted McKenzie out of reminiscing. Knowing it was Ethan, she answered softly, "Hi."

"Hi to you, too. That single word sounds so wonderful to me, you can't imagine. I just did surgery on an otherwise healthy and beautiful springer spaniel that had little tumors around her eyes. Poor thing was absolutely miserable and when I finished, I swear she said, 'thank you' in her whimpers."

"You're so good with animals, they're lucky to have you care so much."

"I'm the lucky one. It's so rewarding to see the gratitude in their eyes when I'm able to help their pain. So, what's up with you calling in the middle of the day? Do you miss me so much you can't wait for tonight?"

"I wish that were the case. I'm afraid I have some bad news."

"Can you tell me over the phone or should I come over?"

"I'd love it if you could come over. Can you take the time?"

"Ginny can handle things here; I'll be there in a few."

True to his word, Ethan ran in the back door in seven minutes, and she rushed into his arms. "I miss you already," she cried.

"What do you mean, miss me? Who's going anywhere?"

"I am. There's a crisis in New York and I have to meet with the police. I don't want to go, but I have to." She filled him in on what she knew of the problems.

Disappointment soured Ethan's face, but he grudgingly nodded in understanding.

"How soon are you leaving?" he asked with a sinking heart.

"Already got a seat on the six o'clock to LaGuardia and I'll stay at the Algonquin tonight. I'm not sure what shape my apartment's in, but I'll check that out tomorrow."

With a disappointed sigh he said, "At least I can take you to the airport. I can leave the clinic early and be here before four. Isabella can stay at Mary Jo's."

"I'd love for you to take me. I'll call Mary Jo to go over stuff about my house and Goldie and maybe I can say goodbye to Isabella."

"Any idea how long you'll be gone?"

"Not yet. I have to talk with Tracey at work and let them know I'm leaving, and I've got several more phone calls to make about being away. I haven't talked with Otis yet, and I'll want to go over things with him when I find out what's really going on in New York."

With hope, he said, "You don't sound happy about this either, but maybe it will all work out quickly and you'll be back before we know it."

"I sure hope so. I'm really going to miss you, you know. You've wormed your way into my heart."

"Yeah. I'm afraid it's going to take more than the worming pills I give to puppies to get you out of mine," he said sadly. They kissed tenderly and held each other for not nearly long enough, and then Ethan left for his clinic.

With a deep sigh, McKenzie continued her calls to people at her office, and texted Desirée about her flight and seeing her the next morning at the Ward building. Time didn't allow for sniveling.

◆◆◆◆◆

McKenzie had had a life-long friendship with her childhood buddy, Otis Jorgensen. They hadn't seen each other since she had left for college in New York seventeen years before, after growing up inseparable most of the time, playing ball, hunting crawdads, and sneaking treats from McKenzie's mom or Otis's Gramps. They did everything together, including seventh-grade football, when the coach thought 'Kenny' was a boy.

Seeing Otis again and finally meeting his engaging wife, Mary Jo, and boys, Albert and Ben, was sheer delight when she returned to Deep Lake. In spite of the small-town troubles they got into as kids, Otis had always wanted a career in law enforcement and he had been a Chief Deputy Sheriff of Washington County, with his office located in Deep Lake. Recently, after some help from McKenzie in solving a strange murder case, Otis was made an Assistant Sheriff.

She couldn't catch Otis when she tried, but she called Mary Jo, and as expected, she quickly agreed over the phone to board Goldie while

McKenzie went to New York. McKenzie had grown comfortably close to Otis's wife, so impulsively asked if she could drop by for a chat. It was still early, and she needed the contact.

Mary Jo chuckled and said, "I've got some chocolate chip pecans just coming out of the oven. Can you smell them way over there?"

They lived only a couple of blocks apart in the older part of Deep Lake. McKenzie hadn't planned to go to her office until noon that day, but the call from New York was rapidly changing all plans. "Be over in five minutes. Bring Goldie along?"

"For sure, I'll put the girls in the back yard to play while we talk. See ya."

McKenzie clipped on Goldie's leash, put her sneakers back on after their early-morning jog, and headed out the door.

◆◆◆◆◆

"It smells like heaven in here!" McKenzie inhaled the delicious aroma as she quickly knocked and walked in Mary Jo's back door. A plate of her favorites was on the kitchen table and her friend was pouring her a mug of coffee. She had put Goldie in the back yard with their dog, Honey, a litter sister to Goldie. They had already sniffed each other from end to end and were happily racing around the yard.

"Otis at work?"

"Yeah, he left early to meet with the sheriff on something happening in Stillwater. Always something going on, even in this part of the world that we think is so simple."

Otis worked closely with the sheriff at the county government center in Stillwater, a few miles from Deep Lake.

"That's the truth. Crime happens everywhere, and our small town is no exception."

Mary Jo sat down with her own coffee. "Now what's got you riled up, Kenzie, I can see you've got a problem."

"You're right," McKenzie thoughtfully nibbled on her cookie. "I don't know what I did to be so lucky as to have friends like you and Otis. I haven't known a woman who doesn't work away from home and also bakes cookies, since my mother died. Thank you for being here."

"You know we're always here for you, Kenzie. Now what's bothering you?"

"I have to go back to New York. It's so awful!"

Mary Jo quietly waited for McKenzie to continue.

"A woman was found dead in the office and condo building I own in Manhattan. It sounds like I need to work with the police to find out how she got there, and I don't know what else."

"That's not good. Otis told me you still had business dealings in the East, but I didn't know what it was. It sounds complicated."

"That it is. To be honest, I've been thinking of selling the building because my life seems to be settling more and more in Deep Lake. I've been gone from there for almost a year now, and this is home to me. My manager takes care of things by keeping offices and condos leased and such, but it's a lot of work to keep updating and dealing with security and all. I do make money on the building, but it costs a lot, too, and the way things are going here, I was thinking of putting it on the market. Now, this happened and I have to go there to help decide what to do about it. What a mess," she sighed. "I wish Otis could come with me and take care of the details. He's so good at that."

"Yes, he is, and the two of you worked together so well when your father was murdered, not to mention that awful business this past winter. But don't look at it like that. You've got people there who can help, and maybe it won't be so bad after all. You know we'll look after Goldie and check on your house as long as it takes. You have friends at work here too, who can take care of things, right?"

"Yes, I do, and you're right. I made the right move, going with a local real estate company. My friends will take care of everything. I am so lucky to have all of you. I'll miss everyone and especially Ethan and Isabella, but I have to go, there's no alternative. There's no way to tell how long it will be, either. I've got an open-ended ticket and will call about when I can come back."

"See? You're already making plans and that's what you're best at."

"I don't know about 'best,' but I do like to have a plan. I'd better go home and make some more calls because I'm going out there tonight. I'll try to call Otis, too."

"I'm sure he will be eager to hear from you—you know how he loves a mystery. Why don't you just leave Goldie here now? The boys can take the wagon over later to pick up her food and bowls and whatever toys she likes. You know we all love her." She continued, "Wait a minute, Isabella comes here after school anyway, how about if she comes with Albert and Ben to get Goldie's things. They should be there about three. Then you can say goodbye to her."

"Good idea. You know, I don't like that term, goodbye—it sounds so permanent and for some reason, it's scary."

"Then don't say it. Say instead, 'I'll see you soon.'"

"You're right as always. See you soon," and McKenzie gave Mary Jo a tight hug and ran out the door.

◆◆◆◆◆

Back at home, she called Otis who was in his office. "You're leaving for New York? So, what's going on, Kenzie, got another murder you need me to solve?" he asked kiddingly.

"Hmm, I sure do wish you were going with me—there *is* a dead body there."

"Whoa, what's going on? You know I was just ribbing you, don't cha?"

"Yeah. They found a dead woman in an abandoned office in my building. I have to talk with the police about it and see if they can find out who she was and what happened. I'm not doing any sleuthing, so don't worry."

"Are you shittin' me, Kenzie? You know you'll start nosing around; you can't help it—it's in your nature. And I won't be there to keep you out of trouble…What does Ethan think about this?"

"He's not happy, as you can guess. He's coming soon to take me to the airport. You know I'm gonna miss all of you, but I have to go, that's all there is to it."

"Oh boy, you'll call or text me from New York, right? Let me know what's happening so I can help you talk through it and keep you out of trouble. I'll keep an eye on Ethan and Isabella for you; they're gonna miss you, too."

"Thanks, Otis. I'll keep in touch and you'll be the first to know if I solve another crime."

♦♦♦♦♦

Before she knew it, three o'clock came and the back doorbell rang. Looking out the door, she saw Albert and Ben with their red wagon, and Isabella was looking sad. The moment she opened the door, the tearful little girl ran into her arms. "Mary Jo said you were going away!"

After comforting the child who already occupied a big part of her heart, she said, "Oh, Isabella, I'm afraid it's true. I have to go back to New York City to take care of some urgent business. I wish I didn't have to go, but I must."

"Are you ever coming back?" Isabella asked uncertainly, and Albert and Ben tried to look stoic as they all waited for McKenzie's reply.

"Of course I'm coming back, you silly goose! How could I ever leave this happy place forever?" The children all gave a sigh of relief.

Albert took the lead and said, "We're glad, Kenzie. Isabella would really miss you." They all nodded in unison.

"I'm not exactly sure how long I'll be gone, though. This business might take a while to fix, but for sure, I'll be back. You can count on it."

They loaded up in the wagon the supplies for Goldie, and amid smiles and waves and the comforting knowledge that their much-loved Kenzie would come back to them, the three youngsters headed toward the Jorgensen home.

Gathering her travel bags and keeping busy to avoid her own tears, Ethan arrived minutes later and the two of them drove to the MSP Airport almost in silence.

When they came to the Delta departure door, they sat in the car and held each other until other cars around them were honking for him to get moving. With false smiles, they gave promises of calls and texts, and McKenzie pulled reluctantly out of Ethan's arms, swept through the doors, and headed for her gate.

CHAPTER 2
ARRIVING BACK IN NEW YORK CITY

McKenzie looked out over New York City as her plane was landing at LaGuardia Airport. It was impressive, to be sure, with small and tall buildings packed closely together to serve the complex lives of more than eight million people.

"Skyscraper National Park." That's what Kurt Vonnegut famously labeled New York City in his novel, *Slapstick*. With more than 700,000 buildings in the city, it was forever in a perpetual state of renewing, restructuring, removing, and rebuilding.

One of those 700,000 buildings belonged to McKenzie Ward. She had been a successful Commercial Realtor in "The Big Apple," for almost fifteen years and was able to acquire, with her father's help, an office and condo building. A small one, only eight stories, but a building in Manhattan, nonetheless. It was built in the 1930s, located on Park Avenue with an almost-view of the East River, and between the river and Central Park. Called the Ward Building, it had small and large businesses located on the first three floors, along with parking below ground. The upper floors were condominium homes, and both her business office and her apartment were in the building. She thought the building was as secure as she could make it, but from the sound of Desirée's phone call it was apparent that was no longer the case.

◆◆◆◆◆

After landing at LaGuardia, McKenzie headed for the ground transportation area to find a taxi. She hadn't checked any baggage and hoped against hope that her carry-on held what she'd need for the time she was there. As she was ready to hail a taxi, she suddenly heard her name being called. Turning in surprise, she saw her former boyfriend, Michael Romano, striding toward her.

She and Michael had parted on less-than-friendly terms when she moved back to Deep Lake, after dating exclusively, or so she thought, for several years. Tall and dark with a commanding presence, Michael was handsome and charming. A successful and powerful attorney, Michael had been a wonderful and attentive date, and an occasional captivating lover. They had never talked about marriage and McKenzie learned later that he dated other women all along, with whom he had equally close relationships.

Seeing him now after almost a year, was a shock. "Michael, what are you doing here?"

"Welcome back, McKenzie. New York has missed you and so have I. You're as beautiful as ever, in fact, even more, I have to tell you. I've already got a taxi just over here to take you to the Algonquin," he said as he took her bag.

"You knew I was coming tonight? And you know where I'm staying?" she questioned as they walked to the taxi.

"I talked with Desirée and heard about the troubles in the Ward Building. Just thought I'd make your arrival a little easier. I've really missed you, you know. I owe you a huge apology for how I acted when you left everything here to move to the sticks, I mean Minnesota. I couldn't believe you were really leaving me. You meant more to me than you realize then and now, McKenzie. I am so sorry about what happened, and I'll do everything I can to help you believe I really care about you."

Zooming along New York streets, McKenzie was overwhelmed with this unexpected outburst. In their former connection, the word "sorry" was nonexistent in Michael's vocabulary. Any faux pas he might be caught at was invariably passed off with innate charm and smooth discourse.

"Michael, this is so unexpected. I thought our relationship was over when I left the city. I have to tell you I am now involved with another man in Deep Lake, and things are looking very committed with this relationship."

"Committed. It sounds like you've gone a little weird since you left us. I've missed you so much. Let's have a drink at that little bar we liked in SoHo. It's still early and I can drop you at the Algonquin later."

"No, Michael. I'm expecting a heavy day tomorrow, and I need some sleep."

"This used to be the shank of the evening before you left. You were really sassy then. Come on, girl, let your hair down, and let's have that drink."

"No, again. I'm going to the hotel and that's final." She moved to the right a little more and put her purse between them as he had been sliding closer and closer.

After a short silence, he said, "I guess you're right. We can catch up tomorrow after you've had a good sleep."

They soon arrived at her hotel and she jumped out, retrieved her bag, and said, "Good night, Michael. Thanks for picking me up. I'll be fine from here on." Shutting the cab door in his face, she almost ran into the hotel giving him no chance to respond.

◆◆◆◆◆

With an easy check-in because of former relationships with the hotel and some of the staff, McKenzie was rewarded with a beautiful room. She collapsed immediately onto the big cushy bed, sighed deeply, and spread out looking at the ceiling. "What have I gotten myself into," she said to herself. She already knew Michael was going to be a problem throughout her stay because of his actions in picking her up from the airport. It was becoming obvious that nothing would stop him from pursuing her, and she could see he was already laying claim to her now that she was back on what he considered "his turf."

When her heart stopped racing and her pulse went to somewhat normal, she determined to curtail his advances with a stronger message to back off starting the next morning if he showed up, which she already knew he would. She had enough to think about with the police investigation and finding out what was happening in her building. She just wasn't feeling right about calling Ethan after her bizarre arrival, so she texted him instead: "Arrived OK, fine flight. Gonna get a good night's sleep before tomorrow. Miss you tons, and kisses to both of you!!"

CHAPTER 3
DARKNESS IN DEEP LAKE

Ethan was missing McKenzie even more than he admitted to her in his reply to her text. The morning was long and filled with routine pet needs, like cleaning out dog and puppy ears, sewing up some cuts, writing a diet for someone's new parrot, and more. The larger animal home visits would be later.

He left his clinic for a lonely lunch at Joe's, the Deep Lake family restaurant where locals gathered. As the hostess showed him to a small booth, he nodded as a cart went by and said, "Hey Timmy, good to see you." Timmy was a busboy at Joe's, a grinning, differently abled young man with Down syndrome. He started working at the restaurant several years before, while he was going to Stillwater high school, and had stolen the hearts of everyone in town. Ethan didn't know Timmy's family but had heard that his mother just showed up one day in town and took a job at the Deep Lake Bank.

A shadow loomed over Ethan's table and he looked up. "Hey Thompson, long time no see." Ethan looked up into the non-smiling eyes of a man who immediately sat down across from him. "Your secretary—she's a looker, that one, you must enjoy your work—told me where to find you."

"Buddy." Ethan choked on the name as he swallowed the first and last bite of his sandwich. The balding, slightly paunchy man kept smiling and Ethan noticed he was missing a couple of significant teeth. Things must not have gone the way the formerly swaggering braggart from high school had hoped.

"Yeah, I wondered where you ran off to when you left town. I've been looking for you. Seems like you've got yourself a sweet little business here. Things going pretty well?"

"What are you doing here, Buddy? You and I have nothing to talk about, and I have no idea why you've been looking for me."

"Whoa there, Ethan. Us Fondy Cardinals need to stick together, right?" Buddy was referring to the high school they both had attended in Fond du Lac, Wisconsin, and graduated in the late 'nineties.

Buddy grabbed a few fries off Ethan's plate. With his mouth full and pointing a fry at Ethan, he sneered, "Remember that little caper you and the other guys pulled right before graduation?"

Ethan paled and his one bite of sandwich turned to stone in his gut. "You were there, too, Buddy, you know what happened."

"Yeah, dude, but I'm not in any of the photos."

"Photos?"

"That's right, photos. I've got a dozen of 'em and you're right in the front. How do you like that, my friend?"

"How?...We all agreed, it was a terrible accident. We didn't know that horse was in the barn. It all got out of hand, Buddy, you know that. We agreed to never tell about being there, and it was all ruled the accident it really was."

Ethan's mind was whirling. He could see the spreading flames after the fire mysteriously got started. No one admitted starting it, and the group of hockey players tried valiantly, but in vain, to stamp it out.

At the end of the hockey season their senior year, he had been pressured to go along with other members of the team to what they thought was an old, abandoned barn outside town to drink some beer. Somebody, and just this moment he remembered that it was Buddy, had brought along some weed to smoke—although Ethan had been too cautious to smoke any of it. The boys were just hanging out together laughing and rehashing the former season with the ins, outs, and foibles of every game played. The sudden and terrifying screams of an old horse in back of the barn shocked them all, and they ran as flames spread and quickly engulfed the tinder-dry structure. Ethan was the last to leave as he ran in panic toward the horse to try to free him from the encroaching inferno. He couldn't reach the horse and had to finally stumble outside himself as a couple of the other guys began to drag him out to avoid being caught by the firestorm.

Ethan never recovered from that scene. It also confirmed his path to eventually becoming a veterinarian in the hopes of saving animals like the doomed horse that died in the barn fire.

"Again, Buddy, what photos?"

"You remember my sister got married about then. She had these little cheap cameras on the tables at the party after for people to take pitchers of each other. I pinched a couple. Never knew how handy they would be down the line."

"Why have you waited all this time to do anything about the pictures?"

"That my friend, is why I'm here. I been watching you and the rest of the guys. You got a big scholarship to go to college, and I never did. They said it was because of a DUI or my grades or something, but I know it was all rigged. You got every break there was, man; you even got gorgeous Elizabeth, the gal we all wanted."

"You must know that Elizabeth has died."

"Yeah, I know, but I also know you got a sweet little girl who wouldn't be happy if her darling daddy had to go to prison for starting a fire that killed a horse and burned down a barn. This is gonna cost you some bucks if you know what I mean. Twenty thousand of them … for now."

"You can't mean this, Buddy. Are you saying you'll go to the police with those old photos just to destroy me?" Ethan stood up and grabbed Buddy out of his seat. He clutched Buddy's vest in both hands and said in a deadly whisper, "This is blackmail, plain and simple. I won't have it!"

People around them had been sneaking glances and were watching in full interest when Ethan grabbed Buddy. Buddy pulled away, straightened his shirtfront and said loudly, "Good to see you too, Thompson. I'll be around," and he stalked out of the restaurant.

♦♦♦♦♦

Unknown to Ethan and Buddy, or so she thought, a woman was sitting quietly in the corner of the restaurant and had seen the confrontation between the two men.

The woman was Timmy's mother, Linda, on her lunch break from the bank, and there to keep an eye on her boy as she did now and then. She was so proud of the way Timmy had grown with this job and made so many friends in the town. She had, too, and was happy she moved to Deep Lake. She had known Ethan's grandmother back in Fond du Lac and kept in touch with her. After Ethan and Elizabeth moved to Minnesota to help his grandmother, Linda moved to Deep Lake also, but she kept to herself and never became acquainted with Ethan. Her friendship with his grandmother was only between the two of them and when the older woman passed away Linda stayed in the town and with the bank, but away from Ethan. She raised Timmy and made a few friends through her church and work, making a quiet and pleasant life for herself and her boy.

♦♦♦♦♦

Buddy had been surprised to see his former wife in the restaurant as he was looking around for Ethan. He had stood in the doorway and recognized her even with her few physical changes before his encounter with Ethan but made no move toward her. "So this is where she ran to," he thought. He didn't think she ever divorced him that he knew about, so she was still his wife. That needed thinking about, but first he must confront Ethan.

CHAPTER 4
THE FIRST DAY BACK IN NYC

After a fitful sleep, McKenzie woke early, knowing she needed a good run to start the day. She and her dog, Goldie ran together at home in Deep Lake and loved their time in the early hours of their small town. McKenzie had a mapped-out route that gave them a good three-mile run most mornings. Back in New York, after donning her running clothes, she headed for Central Park where she had started her routine of morning outings several years before. As before, she waited for a gap in the crush of puffing New Yorkers in various states of fitness and non-fitness and then joined the herd of grim-faced individuals. None of them, if seemed, really wanted to be there, but were determined to do what was currently recognized as the way to stay healthy.

The smell of dozens of sweating bodies immediately assaulted her and then mingled with the almost forgotten but now remembered ever-present stench of hot garbage. If ever there was a smell associated with The Big Apple, it was garbage. Garbage that had sat all night beside restaurants and bars, festering and rotting while awaiting noisy trucks to haul it away in the morning. Rats chewed holes in plastic bags allowing contents to spill out on sidewalks, and vagrants quickly picked through it looking for anything salvageable. In the summer, the smell bordered on unbearable, but even in the cool spring weather, it never completely went away.

How she missed her pal Goldie and their soul-satisfying early morning sprints in the quiet of their town of clean-smelling air.

Back in her hotel, she showered and dressed in a comfortable but fashionable navy pantsuit and medium heels, in preparation for what was surely to be a long day. She brushed her short blond hair that always fell exactly right now that it was kept up by her friend Janice who owned Sassy Janice's House of Hair in Deep Lake. A chum from high school with whom she reconnected when she moved back to her hometown, Janice was now a close and valued friend. Six feet tall compared to McKenzie's five-eight, Janice was a force to be reckoned with in her no-nonsense approach to life, and her knowledge of human behavior as learned from years of listening to customers in her shop.

McKenzie was missing her at this moment, and also her long-time friend Otis, who would know exactly how to handle the coming interview with the New York police. She and Otis had worked together unofficially to solve both her father's murder and another unexpected killing last winter in Deep Lake. They had been friends from young childhood until McKenzie fled her hometown after her mother's surprising death many years before. She went to college at Cornell University in Ithaca, New York, and after that the commercial real estate world in New York opened up for her. Her youth and naïveté seemed to work to her advantage in the field in the fiercely competitive world of Manhattan commercial real estate and she became surprisingly successful. With her father's help and connections from the judicial bench he served, she was able to buy the Ward Building and continue building her business. Sadness and distress from her mother's strange death—she had been electrocuted in her bathtub—kept her from going home. Her only connection was with her father by phone and his occasional visits. The years went by until she was summoned back to Deep Lake after Judge Ward's death.

Returning now to the life she had left less than a year ago, was nostalgic for sure, and being there brought memories of fun times as well as stressful times. She was startled by discovering she actually missed some of her old life, and the discovery led to guilt about pieces of her new life in Deep Lake.

This nostalgic stage had to end as she needed to get to her former office in the Ward Building to start investigating the problems there. She pulled herself together and grabbed a cab for the short trip instead of walking the few blocks which might have triggered a whole new set of memories.

◆◆◆◆◆

At the front door of the Ward Building, the security guard/doorman opened her cab door and effusively welcomed McKenzie. Bernie Williams had been with the building for many years and had come with the territory when McKenzie acquired it. He hadn't changed a minute since she saw him last. Tall and slightly portly with previously graying hair which she noticed now was carefully colored, Bernie wore his doorman's uniform proudly. It was navy blue with gold braid and included white gloves and black shoes polished to a mirrored shine. He stepped forward and tipped his matching hat, saying, "Miss Ward, I'm so happy to see you! It's been way too long since you've been here."

"Thank you, Bernie. It's good to see you, too. I understand we have an issue here, and I expect you've already dealt with the police."

"I have, miss. It's terrible and I'm so glad you are here now to take care of things."

"I'll try, Bernie, I'll try." And McKenzie stepped into the open elevator and rose to her office on the third floor.

Her former secretary and now Desirée's, Gayle Granville, had started with McKenzie when she was an unknown and beginning Commercial Realtor. They hugged in mutual respect and fondness for their long-time working relationship. Gayle handled the office needs and supervised all the paperwork, and McKenzie noticed a couple of new people who were busy at their computers. Desirée had already made a few changes in the business and had obviously needed more help.

Gayle had pictures on her desk of a new grandchild and proudly announced that her first grand now called her "GeeGee." Gayle hardly looked grandmotherly in her stylish dress and sleek hairdo, but McKenzie remembered their mutual joy when that first grand was born a couple of years before.

"Oh Gayle, where does the time go? You still look terrific, dear, and I think Desirée keeps you busy here."

"That she does, McKenzie, that she does. Things are different without you here, but most definitely busy. And here she is now."

Clicking down the wooden-floored hallway in Ferragamo coral-colored boots, a bright coral leather skirt, and a gorgeous silk jacket top, Desirée looked stunning. Her glorious dark brown hair with reddish highlights was done in an undercut style that swung over one eye. "McKenzie, you look great," she gushed as she kissed both of her cheeks. "The country air seems to be agreeing with you, but it's so good to see you back in your domain."

"Thank you, Desirée, I have to return the compliment, and I think that business must be good from what I'm seeing so far."

"Good, yes, and we can talk more about it later. We need to get this trouble taken care of first. Let's go to my office as I bring you up to date. The detective will be here in an hour, so you need to know what's happening."

They started down the hall when Desirée stopped and said, "Two coffees, Gayle, in my office. My usual, and you should remember how McKenzie likes hers."

"Yes, Desirée, right away." Gayle looked at McKenzie and they were both remembering the days when McKenzie usually made the coffee and served Gayle as she frantically typed out contracts and closing papers for the latest commercial deal. Times had changed.

The corner office that used to be McKenzie's had already been sumptuously redesigned according to Desirée's opulent French tastes, and they both sank into soft cushions on the royal blue leather sofa. The rest of the room was done in bright colors with the sofa as the centerpiece. Large windows reflected early spring outside, but the views were mainly of other taller buildings, as they had been when McKenzie looked out of them the previous spring.

"Do you like the decorating?" Desirée asked proudly. "I hope you don't mind that I moved in as long as you weren't going to be here. I've kept the adjoining office for your use while you're here. It should be large enough, and your furniture has been moved there."

"I know that office, certainly, and it's beautiful. How could I not like it? You have exquisite taste, and all I need is a place where I can put my purse in a drawer and sit a minute."

"Thank you, McKenzie. When you asked me to take things over for you here, I admit I was thrilled. Things have really been going very well until we hit this glitch in the building."

"Tell me what happened so I can get on board before the detective arrives. I don't know what to expect at this point."

"Of course. As you know, we have parking on the below-ground floors for tenants, but few of our residents have their own cars. The businesses use some spots, but our garage isn't always terribly busy, which is similar to other buildings like ours in Manhattan. We still have to maintain it and keep up our security. Tenants have key cards to use on the garage and side doors, and of course, Bernie is on duty in the front during the day and he likes to work six days a week. We have another man who works evenings, but between nine p.m. and seven a.m., and on Sundays, tenants use their key cards to get in the building. The maintenance man, Tony Wosika, is still here, and I think you hired him years ago." McKenzie nodded. "He says he hasn't seen anything unusual in the building, but he's busy all the time and most of the time has his head buried under somebody's sink."

"We've handled things this way as long as I've owned the building," McKenzie said.

"Yes, I know, but somehow it's not working now. An import-export business moved out on the second floor and things got sticky."

"Sticky?"

"Well, we thought the business was doing well because of the amount of traffic they did with trucks coming and going, huge cartons and even heavy metal ship containers of stock being loaded and unloaded in the basement garage. All of a sudden, the activity seemed to stop, and nobody even noticed that the trucks weren't coming anymore. Apparently, they sort of sneaked out in the middle of the night. By the time we realized they were not conducting business anymore, all of their inventory was gone and the offices were completely empty. No one realized what was happening, and we haven't been able to find them since then."

"And?"

"As I said, we didn't realize their spot was empty for a while and some druggies must have got hold of their key cards. We finally found out they've been going in and out by the side doors."

"So, you changed the key cards right away, right?"

"Yes, of course we did, but that didn't solve the problem. We're really in a bad spot right now, and I'm not sure what to do."

"When was the woman found?"

"Three days ago. A gal from another business on second floor went looking around when they noticed a bad smell coming from that area. The front door was open and she found the woman on the floor. It was gross for everyone."

McKenzie's head was spinning as she tried to take in all of the information when Gayle knocked and stuck her head in the office. "The detective is here."

"Bring him back here," Desirée answered.

The detective was there in moments and introduced himself as Detective Lieutenant Miguel Garcia. He was dressed in a decent-looking suit, and McKenzie oddly noticed his shoes were shined. She couldn't help remembering her mother had told her to always look at a man's shoes. "Men take care of their wives like they take care of their shoes," she had said when McKenzie was quite small. She found this memory comforting as she met the serious dark-haired man who had a slight Latino accent. He was tall with ruggedly handsome good looks.

Garcia began, "I've been working with Ms. Canard, but she said you are the owner of the building, Ms. Ward."

"I am. However, I've moved to Minnesota over the past year and Ms. Canard has been managing my business interests here in New York."

"I'm presuming she has updated you on what happened here. Have you seen where the woman was found in the building?"

"No, but I would like to."

"Follow me," and he walked toward the door. "I'd like to talk with you alone if that is agreeable. We've already interviewed Ms. Canard and Mrs. Granville."

Desirée said, "Please do go ahead with Detective Garcia, McKenzie. He's already becoming familiar with our building and he knows what to look for."

◆◆◆◆◆

McKenzie, who of course already knew every inch of the Ward Building, followed Garcia to the elevator. They didn't speak until they got off on the second floor. She took a quick in-breath when she saw the crime scene tape on the door of Suite 2D but entered along with the detective as he unlocked the door.

The previous tenant had operated an import-export business for furniture and art objects. They had leased their offices the year before when McKenzie was still active in her business. In fact, she remembered buying some small art pieces from them that were eye-catching and unusual. The owner said they were from South America but didn't get more specific than that.

She remembered the owner, a small and thin Spanish man named Mateo Robles, who dressed impeccably. Even so, he exuded a sort of oiliness about him; a silly word to use, she thought, but she had always felt uneasy around him because he seemed to be a little too perfect in his speech and appearance. She knew by instinct she would never really trust Mr. Robles. The way things looked at that moment, her distrust was well-earned and she realized she had been too hasty when trying to fill the large space.

McKenzie and Detective Garcia stood in the middle of the big empty area, each distracted by their separate thoughts.

Garcia then moved toward a pile of blankets in a corner, next to a row of cubicles. "This is where the young woman was found."

McKenzie looked at the dirty and foul-smelling blankets that covered a thin mat on the floor, and her heart broke as she speculated about how the girl had come to be there and what might have happened in her life to bring her to where she was found.

Lost in her thoughts, Garcia startled her by saying, "I can tell you, Miss Ward, that after some investigation, this does not look like an 'ordinary' drug overdose death. I'm sorry to use the word 'ordinary' in such a casual way; please be assured we are approaching this in anything but a casual manner."

"I understand, Detective Garcia. How sad that you even have to qualify the death of a young person in such terms. Tell me what you know about the girl. How did she get in here? Why did she pick this building? And where did she come from?"

"Whoa, that's a little more than I can tell you right now."

"Sorry, this is hard for me. I recently lost my father as well as another family member who was close to me, and I may have a more expanded outlook on the value of life at this point in my own life."

"It's a wise way to look at it, Ms. Ward."

"Call me McKenzie, please."

"I will, and you can call me Detective, or just Garcia as I'm known to most. We may be seeing more of each other in the next few weeks than you know."

"Weeks? I was hoping this wouldn't take more than a few days."

"From the results of our initial investigation and the preliminary autopsy of the young girl, we're looking at a deeper level of examination of exactly the questions you are asking. I think we're done here for now, but I'll need to talk with you further, maybe some time tomorrow. Your cell phone is?"

She gave him her number and they left the office space. McKenzie suspected it was feeling oppressive for both of them. Garcia left the building and she went back to her "new" office to think.

◆◆◆◆◆

McKenzie had hardly sat down when her cell buzzed. She saw it was Ethan calling and picked up eagerly. "Hello, my darling, I'm so glad you called."

"I miss you. Deep Lake seems already empty without you here."

"That's sweet of you to say but I've been gone only less than a day."

"It seems like a week, at least. Isabella went to bed in a really glum mood last night. She prayed for you to come home quickly."

"I miss both of you, you know I do. Speaking of that, I don't know how long I'll be here. I spoke with the detective this morning and he didn't sound too hopeful that this would be quickly solved. Not sure why."

"That's not good news. I've gotten so accustomed to having you in our lives, I really miss you. Please remember how much you're loved and don't let anything happening there mess with that." He gave a big sigh. "We'll keep things going until you get back."

"I remember, and I always will. I love you, too."

They ended the call, with reluctance on both parts.

CHAPTER 5
DEEP LAKE WITHOUT MCKENZIE

The phone call with McKenzie was distressing to Ethan. He knew he had come to depend on her sunny disposition to fuel his own. The years since his wife, Elizabeth, had died were filled with work and expanding his clinic, and parenting Isabella. He had learned quickly that having a daughter was not just a part-time job, and losing his wife with Isabella only a tiny baby was brutal.

He had greatly missed Elizabeth and her willingness to share the world they had built together. Their marriage had been close and familiar, and losing her to a horribly painful cancer death was indescribable. He never expected to fall in love again, and for years had resisted the lovely young women his friends and family subtly and not so subtly brought around to meet him.

McKenzie had changed his view. From the first time he saw her sitting in the waiting room of his clinic, he was drawn to her beauty and openness. The daughter of his recently deceased fishing buddy, Judge Arthur Ward, he was suspicious when McKenzie brought the judge's dog in with cut feet. Ethan knew right away the cuts were human-inflicted and didn't want this to be the work of the judge's daughter. He learned quickly she was not guilty, and began working with her and their mutual friend, Otis Jorgensen, on solving a complicated case that involved the dog's injury and more.

Ethan and McKenzie became closer and closer as time passed. Her bright mind and positive outlook on life drew him as no other woman ever had. She was interested in political discussions and made points that showed thought and common sense, which delighted him. They didn't always agree, and that just brought on more discussion and sharing of views, to stimulate both of them.

His adorable and brilliant little girl was drawn immediately to McKenzie's warmth and genuine interest in others, and the three of them were quickly and seriously becoming a family. Or so he thought. He knew McKenzie had been involved with a man in New York before she came back to Deep Lake, but she wasn't completely open about her relationship with him. Michael was his name and he was a high-powered attorney. Ethan tried to delicately inquire now and then about how involved the two of them might have been, but without success. She had tried to assure him that her relationship with Michael was over, but now that she was back in New York for this investigation over the death of someone in her building, he was nervous about whether she might be open to getting back together with Michael.

Ethan hadn't told McKenzie about the meeting at Joe's with his former hockey team member, Buddy. The conversation was so disagreeable, and he was embarrassed at his own anger when Buddy went so far as to threaten him with blackmail. He planned to tell her about the situation and the full story of the barn fire when he was able to calm down—most likely when she came back from New York. It wasn't the type of thing he wanted to talk about on the phone. He was still upset about Buddy's threat and didn't know if he would come back to cause more trouble or not. It was a bad memory and one that had the possibility of causing great disruption of Ethan's life. He was having a hard time thinking about how he would handle things if Buddy did show up again.

The very thought of Buddy having pictures of that long-ago fire burned his insides. After hearing Buddy talk about that, he had trouble thinking of anything else. In fact, that afternoon when he went out to deal with a cow with digestive problems, he could hardly stay involved with what was happening. The farmer even asked him if he was feeling okay.

After the call with McKenzie, he collapsed on his bed contemplating the happenings of a terrible day, and desperately wished he could feel his arms around her right that minute.

CHAPTER 6
RECONNECTING WITH NYC

Thinking about her visit to Suite 2D with Detective Garcia, McKenzie decided to do a walk-around the building by herself. She was eager to check out her own apartment on the top floor, but first spent a couple of hours just walking the halls and checking in with her business tenants. A few were new and had moved in after she left the city, but the majority were people she had leased or sold space to, and some had been friends for many years. She stopped by some of them, including the jewelry shop with its hand-designed silver specialties, the collection agency, the beauty shop, the India clothing boutique, and more. Feeling comforted by pleasant reunions, and happy to see that most were operating successfully, she continued her way down the building.

A busy restaurant, Patisserie Alain, featured French pastries, including croissants to die for, took up much of the first floor, and they were gearing up for the lunch crowd. McKenzie greeted the owner and the maître d' but didn't stay around to get in the way of customers. Depending on how her time went that week, she might have dinner there with Gayle and Desirée.

Sara Hutton owned the flower shop next to the building's main entrance. She supplied flowers for the lobby and they always looked terrific. Bernie, the doorman, picked them up daily along with a scarlet carnation for his lapel. McKenzie stood in the middle of Sara's shop, closed her eyes and inhaled the jumbled saccharine scent of roses, lilies, daisies, peonies,

Sweet William, and more. All were punctuated by the simple earthy smell of good black dirt pressed in pots of bright gerbera daisies, tulips, and spring bulb garden baskets. Big containers of early spring daffodils stood by the entrance to the shop, and Sara handed each customer a small bunch as a gift as they left. She handed McKenzie several bunches after their happy reunion hug. Sara told her, "It's so good to see you again. We've missed your smile. I hope these pretty daffodils will help to brighten up your office after being away so long."

"Thank you, Sara. I'm thrilled to see you're doing so well in your beautiful shop. You've added a great line of gifts that I'm eager to look at more closely, and your flowers are always the freshest."

"You're too kind, McKenzie." She continued in a more serious vein, "I expect you're getting the lowdown about the death in the building. Is that what brought you back?"

"Yes, I'm afraid so. It's a bad business, and I feel so sad for that young girl."

"We do, too. We've all given statements already to that detective and his team about anything we've seen. In my case, that's pretty much nothing. I don't have a lot of connection with other tenants other than to sell them flowers. Bernie keeps me up to date on what's going on. How long will you be here?"

"Good question. I have no idea at this point. Detective Garcia is working on things but I do need to be here for a while."

"How is Minnesota? Are you really thinking of staying there? It's hard for me to imagine you anywhere but New York. I've never been there, but is it really as cold and backwoods there as M…people say?"

Catching Sara's slip of the tongue and knowing it was Michael that Sara was referring to, she answered, "No, not really. Some people have the wrong idea."

Feeling a little offended, McKenzie clutched her flowers, left the store and decided it was time to check out her apartment.

◆◆◆◆◆

The elevator whooshed McKenzie up to the eighth floor, and in moments she was facing the door to 8A. Memories of her decision to make this apartment her home wrapped around her like the soft blankets with which she surrounded herself when spending any length of time there. Softness was what she craved after the long demanding days of her work, and she had totally decorated her space with soft pillows, plush carpets, filmy curtains, and cushy lap robes. Colors were gentle with comforting ivories, blues, and greens. Now she eagerly turned her key in the door to return to the softness she longed for.

The woman she hired to periodically clean her apartment was trustworthy and McKenzie expected it to be as she had left it. Instead, the first thing that dominated her view when entering was a huge and garish bouquet of blinding colors in a monstrous crystal vase that dwarfed her delicate antique coffee table.

Michael. It could only be Michael, and she understood Sara's almost slip with his name when she made her cutting comment about McKenzie's home state. He must have just ordered the flowers.

Against her practicality, but in keeping with her heart, she smashed the flowers, vase and all, in her trash basket.

"How *dare* he do this!" she hissed to herself. "He invaded my personal space to leave his mark. And after I've told him repeatedly that our relationship is over!"

Frustrated and furious, she kicked off her shoes, shed her jacket and flopped on her couch. Taking deep breaths, she sank into the softness and held a puffy pillow close to her chest. She struggled with thoughts about how she could deal with what was happening with the girl's death and the police involvement, Michael's invasive behavior, and on top of it all, how much she was missing Ethan. Her mind was whirling, and before she knew it, she fell into a troubled sleep.

◆◆◆◆◆

Jerking awake to her buzzing cell, McKenzie was at first disoriented, and soon realized where she was and why. She answered on the fifth ring, giving herself a moment to fully wake up.

"Oh, there you are, McKenzie. I was beginning to think I'd missed you," Gayle said. "Michael Romano is here in the office and wants to see you. Are you nearby?"

"I'm in my apartment, Gayle, but please don't tell Michael that. Just say I'll be there in a few minutes. He can wait."

◆◆◆◆◆

McKenzie took her time freshening up. While running a brush through her short and wavy blond hair, she couldn't help thinking about her close friend Janice, who kept McKenzie's hair looking good. She hoped that she'd be back in Deep Lake before her next haircut was needed, but more than that, she missed her friend and her sharp wit. Janice had a no-nonsense outlook on life and often reminded McKenzie that too frequently she had her head in the sky. Janice would know the perfect comeback for Michael's aggressiveness, and she nodded to herself.

Her friend Otis would know how to deal with Detective Garcia, also, she knew, and longed for his presence. Unfortunately, she was on her own for this one.

◆◆◆◆◆

When McKenzie stepped into her business reception area, Michael was pacing the floor and talking on his cell. Gayle rolled her eyes.

As soon as he saw McKenzie head toward her new office without giving him a glance, he cut off his call and followed. She sat at her desk and he came in, softly closing the door.

"I was surprised to see the flowers you left. Unfortunately, the vase left a water ring on my antique coffee table. When I tried to move the heavy vase, it slipped out of my fingers and smashed on the floor. How did you get in, by the way?"

"Desirée saw me with the flowers and took me up. I didn't see where else to leave them so I put them on the coffee table. I was hoping that you would have dinner with me tonight so we can talk about everything that's been going on and mostly about how much I've missed you."

While McKenzie specifically didn't thank him for the flowers, he didn't apologize for the water ring. Typical. Michael had an aversion to the word "sorry," as she had long known. She replied, "Yes, Michael, I will have dinner with you tonight. I don't have other plans and it's already after five. We have a number of things to talk about; in particular, our non-relationship."

"I have my car in your garage downstairs but thought we might go to one of our favorite places from…before. We can just take a cab to Nick's. Is that okay?"

Remembering enjoyable evenings together alone or with associates, she decided the quirky atmosphere at Nick's would be good to have a serious talk without rancor.

"Nick's it is. I'll meet you at the door downstairs at seven." Deliberately picking up her phone, she dismissed him, saying, "I have to make some calls now, I'll see you later," and started dialing.

CHAPTER 7

TROUBLE IN DEEP LAKE

Otis's cell rang as he was leaving home for his office. Seeing his friend's name on the readout, he answered, "Yeah, Ethan, it's early, everything okay?"

"No, Otis, it's not. I just got to my clinic this morning and it looks like we've had a break-in. The back door is broken and things have been tossed around. You'd better come over right away if you can."

"Of course, I can—this doesn't sound good. Don't touch anything and wait for me outside."

"Will do, thanks Otis."

Getting to the clinic on Main Street took Otis only moments. Ethan was standing on the sidewalk with his hands in his pockets and looking glum. His clinic assistant, Ginny, was standing nearby, having just arrived for work.

After a cursory look inside the broken door and seeing shards of glass on the floor, Otis asked Ethan, "Do you keep many drugs here?"

"It's all stuff for animals, but, yes, I guess you'd say there are drugs here."

Otis then called the county sheriff. "Gary, I think you need to get over here with me in Deep Lake. Ethan Thompson's vet clinic has been broken into overnight. I haven't checked thoroughly yet, but there could be some drugs missing."

"The guy on Main Street?"

"That's the one."

"On my way and I'll bring a deputy along."

♦♦♦♦♦

Otis and the sheriff looked through the damage inside the clinic as the deputy checked outside. It was apparent the thief or thieves looked for money and left drawers and cabinet doors open and hanging. The locked drug cabinet was pretty much destroyed with vials and containers joining other equipment strewn around the clinic. The floor was a mess with broken glass and unknown liquids in puddles here and there. The animal cages were smashed and empty. Only one small dog had been there when the break-in occurred and it was gone. Ethan didn't look forward to notifying the owner.

Sheriff Walker stood with crossed arms in the middle of the rubble. "You've got a real mess here, Ethan. Can you tell yet if anything is missing?"

Head hanging and in a wearied voice, Ethan answered, "It's hard at this point," looking around at the jumble of broken glass and crumpled chairs and cabinets. "I'm afraid they got some drugs and needles. We keep them in the upper locked cupboard, and I can see that some are not where they should be."

Otis asked, "Who has keys for the drug cabinet, and for the doors, as well?"

"I do, of course, and my clinic helper, Ginny Sherwood. She has a door key because she sometimes gets here before I do. She also has a key for the drug cabinet because she helps to load my bag for farm visits. I don't always know what sort of issues there might be when I go out. We have only those two sets." Ethan was thinking it was a good thing he made a habit of taking his bag with him when he went home each night, as there were drugs and needles in there, also.

Looking around, he continued while shaking his head, "It looks like somebody took a ball bat or a heavy club to do this much damage. Keys don't matter much when somebody wants something this badly."

Both Otis and Sheriff Walker nodded as they looked around again.

Walker called his deputy in to start looking for fingerprints along with Otis. He told the others, "It's probably a lost cause, but we'll see if we can find any prints. The rest of you go home and stay where I can get ahold of you. It could have been kids, and they don't always think about wearing gloves. Ethan, you should call somebody to board up the back door and broken windows when we're done here so nothing else goes missing. It's gonna take a while to clean this up."

Nodding lethargically, Ethan sighed. Ginny was crying and her blond hair was stuck in the tears on her face in blotches as she stood, bending farther and farther to the sidewalk in her misery. He said gently, "Go on home, Ginny. I'll let you know when we can get back in business. The appointment book is gone, but I have some notes in my phone, and I'll let the patients know their appointments are cancelled for now."

◆◆◆◆◆

As Ethan dragged himself home, he felt like the old iconic character Joe Btfsplk created by Al Capp in the Lil Abner comic strip that his father used to laugh about. Joe had a black cloud over his head that symbolized his perpetual bad luck. Was this bad luck for Ethan, or was someone deliberately trying to hurt him? His mind was confused and jumbled. What was he going to do now?

When he got home, he tried calling McKenzie but she didn't answer. He left a message for her to call him ASAP. He missed her dreadfully.

When he stopped later at Mary Jo's to pick up Isabella, he had already called his former mother-in-law in Edina. Isabella would stay with her Grandma Jane for a few days while he got things cleaned up at the clinic.

The drive to deliver his sweet daughter to Jane Rostad's house was silent while he brooded and Isabella tried to understand this new version of her normally happy father.

CHAPTER 8
UNWANTED ADVANCES IN NYC

The elevator doors opened in the lobby of the Ward Building at precisely seven o'clock, and without realizing what was happening, McKenzie stepped out into the waiting arms of tall and darkly handsome Michael Romano. This was most definitely not her intent, but Michael held her tightly and leaned down to kiss her cheek.

"I've been wanting to do this for as long as you've been gone, McKenzie. You feel so right in my arms. It's like you've finally come home where you belong."

Unaccustomed to this sort of behavior by the man she left behind when she moved to Minnesota, McKenzie struggled to free herself.

"Michael, please let me go. I'm afraid that my memories of our parting early last summer are not the same as yours seem to be."

"Maybe not, but I really missed you after you left. I came to understand that you meant more to me than I realized at the time. I've changed, McKenzie, really changed, and I've been waiting to tell you how much I care about you."

Curtly turning out of his embrace, McKenzie said, "Telling is not showing, Michael, and from what I've seen so far, you haven't changed at all. Our taxi is waiting and so is dinner. Let's go," and she walked purposefully across the lobby and out the front door.

◆◆◆◆◆

Dinner was pleasant, after all. McKenzie was comfortable and pleased to be back at Nick's, one of her favorite Italian restaurants. The host even remembered her and said, "Good evening, Mr. Romano, and Ms. Ward, how nice to see you. It's been a long time."

"Yes, Angelo, it's good to be here. Your angel hair pasta has been calling me," she laughed.

It was obvious that Michael had a favorite table, and they were immediately escorted to it. Small talk preceded their dinner, which was as mouth-wateringly delicious as she remembered. The sauce on her scallops and angel hair pasta was as smooth as heaven and was enhanced by the pairing of an excellent champagne that slipped down easily.

She began by emphasizing her need to lessen their contact and his unwanted attentions but was mellowed by the food and more by the champagne he kept pouring. Their table talk became more intimate as Michael pressed her for more details about her life in Minnesota. Somehow, her relationship with Ethan seemed farther away than only miles. It was hard for McKenzie to imagine him in New York, and it was difficult to talk about him, especially with Michael. She had spent so many years in the city, and evenings like this one with Michael were more realistic memories.

Over dessert, as he refilled her champagne glass again, he continued, "My beautiful McKenzie, thank you for dining with me tonight. At last, I see you unwinding from the stresses of your new life and beginning to enjoy being back where you belong. New York and I have missed you so much. It seems so natural to see you across the table from me, and it gives me much pleasure."

With a sigh she answered, "I have to say this does feel good. I was here for a long time, and as my mother used to say, 'old habits die hard.'"

"How about a little walk instead of a cab?"

"That sounds good," she replied as she rose somewhat unsteadily from the table, and he kissed the back of her neck, tenderly. Feeling relaxed, she let herself enjoy the affectionate gesture, instead of rejecting it.

She even let him take her hand as they left the restaurant and started walking, partly to provide balance, but partly because she was remembering and appreciating his strength. Mutual acquaintances became the topic of conversation and she caught up on the trials and tribulations of her former friends. Michael was a wellspring of information on everyone they knew, it seemed, and they laughed together as he filled her in on their activities and whereabouts.

"Whatever happened with Mavis, your old flame?"

"Dear Mavis left us for Washington, I'm afraid. She became caught up in the political life and went there to chase some new adventures. Last I heard she was shagging a congressman and doing some lobbying. It suits her style," he chuckled.

"For sure," she answered with a small giggle. Remembering her own jealousy regarding Mavis who seemed to regularly throw herself at Michael in their former lives, made her giggle more.

"You never needed to be jealous of Mavis, you know. She was never anything more than a diversion for me. I'm sorry now that I didn't tell or show you more strongly how I felt about you."

He stopped walking and turned her toward him to look down into her face. "McKenzie, I've missed you more than I can ever make you understand. I want to make it up to you now, and I hope more than anything that it's not too late."

Touched but confused by this side of Michael that she'd never seen or appreciated before, she didn't know how to respond. Instead, she continued to look intensely into his dark eyes, as he slowly bent to kiss her. She felt her inhibitions melt away as she leaned into him in remembered passion, and the kiss deepened for both of them.

Suddenly embarrassed at her loss of control, McKenzie turned and started walking again and Michael rushed to catch up. She was glad he couldn't see her blushing face as she sputtered, "I shouldn't have let that happen. I-I need to focus on why I'm here."

They soon reached the Ward building and she hurriedly dashed in the door while using a sideways glance to thank him for dinner. With no more than that curt goodbye, she left him staring after her as she ran for the elevator.

♦♦♦♦♦

Later, in the comforting surroundings of her apartment, she fell into her bed with pangs of guilt and regret. "How could I have let myself be so easily dragged back into Michael's arms," she said quietly to herself. Trying to sort out her feelings and deal with what had happened, sleep quickly overcame her exhausted body instead, and she met it with no resistance.

CHAPTER 9
CLINIC DESTROYED IN DEEP LAKE

The night of the break-in provided little sleep, as Ethan paced the hours away trying to determine how to repair his beautiful and efficient animal clinic. Receiving no call from McKenzie made it all worse, as added worries about how she was doing plagued his mind, along with the unanswered question of why she hadn't called as he had asked.

The next morning, with still no call from McKenzie, he called Otis. "Hey, Otis," he began.

"Hey yourself; how are you doing today?"

"Not worth a damn, to be honest."

"Sort of to be expected, don't-cha think? Somebody really did a job on your place."

"Yeah. I was hoping you guys were finished with fingerprints and whatever else you had to do yesterday. I'd like to get started on cleaning things up. I did get someone to board up the door and windows, at least."

"How about you meet me over there in a few, so we can get a clearer look at what might have been taken. The sheriff wants a list so we can get a better handle on what to do about the whole thing."

"Works for me. I'll meet you there in fifteen minutes." Ethan hung up the phone and rubbed his eyes. While he still had his cell in his hand, it rang and he thankfully saw McKenzie's name in the display.

"Kenzie, you finally called!"

"I'm so sorry, Ethan, I had turned my phone off last night and forgot to turn it back on. How's everything in Deep Lake—and what's the ASAP about?"

"Not so good, I'm afraid. My clinic was broken into night before last, and it's a terrible mess."

"Oh, Ethan, that's awful! Was it kids, or do you know who did it?"

"Otis and Sheriff Walker are working on it. Whoever it was broke in the back door and smashed the windows. Actually, they smashed up pretty much the whole place. I'm meeting Otis there in a few minutes to make a list of what's missing. It's gonna be tough."

"That's horrible! Are you okay? I'm so sorry you have to go through this," McKenzie said as tears started.

"I'm okay. I just miss you so much. I wish you were here."

McKenzie's guilt over her dinner the night before with Michael made her stomach roll and she sat down with a shudder. It was an hour later in New York of course, and she was already in her office and awaiting Detective Garcia.

She replied, "I miss you, too, but I'm working with a detective here to try to solve the death in the building, and I can't go home yet."

"I know, we just have to deal with it," he said with dread. "I have to head over to the clinic now to meet Otis, so I'll call you later to talk. Keep your phone on now, will you?"

"That's a given. Please take care of yourself, you know I'll be thinking of you," she said through tears.

"Me, too. I miss you," he said with apprehension fed by agony, and they hung up.

◆◆◆◆◆

The front of the building wasn't too badly damaged as Otis and Ethan looked it over. The intruders came through the back, most likely because it was more protected from view, and as Ethan had mentioned the day before, must have used a heavy club or maybe a metal ball bat to do the smashing. Wearing gloves to protect their hands from glass shards, they focused on the drug cabinet that had already been dusted for fingerprints. Ethan tried to make the required list of missing drugs and equipment, but it was difficult because of the damage. He did the best he could and found that a number of needles and containers of antibiotics and anesthesia drugs were missing.

Otis headed back to his office with the list, after telling Ethan he should wait another day or two with repairs while they tried to work out what had happened and how to deal with the stolen drugs.

Animals are not that much different than people. They have infections and respiratory issues, allergies, broken bones, and cuts and bruises. They also have need for antiparasitic drugs, and especially food animals must have detailed written treatment records in place to decrease the risk of violative residues in meat, milk, or eggs. All patient treatments must be recorded, and Ethan was gratified to see that while his records cabinets were opened and contents thrown around the room, it looked like he might be able to pull things together when he was allowed access to them. Ginny would be a big support with this work, and he knew she would like to help.

Ethan wasn't able to do more at the clinic, so he headed home. He called his former mother-in-law to see how Isabella was faring. Jane lived in Edina, Minnesota, a suburb of Minneapolis. She was a widow whose husband died young, and she moved from Milwaukee when her daughter was sick and decided to stay in the area after Elizabeth died. Isabella loved her grandmother and was fine with staying with her for a few days. She could miss some school this spring without problems, she was only in first grade, but he hoped it would *not* be long before she and McKenzie, too, would be back with him.

He spoke briefly with Isabella and could tell she was confused about why she had to go away. She missed him and also McKenzie because they had been spending a lot of time together. He tried to reassure her, but in total misery himself, it wasn't easy. They hung up with air kisses and I-love-yous, but neither of them was satisfied with their chat.

He missed McKenzie badly. They had grown close quickly after they met, and it felt so natural for him to be with her. He loved eating together in the evenings at his house or hers, playing checkers or some other family game for the three of them. After the death of his wife more than five years before, he never thought he could feel so right in the presence of another woman. Kenzie's laugh could light up the room, and he knew she would comfort him after the misfortune of the break-in. He also knew no phone call could let him feel his arms around her.

He remembered the time they had sneaked away a couple of months before for a weekend in Red Wing at the famous old hotel. Relaxed and alone, they reveled in their new-found love, and the happiness he felt was indescribable for himself, and he believed it was for McKenzie, too. He prayed that she would remember that weekend when she might be tempted by old friends and relationships while she was away.

Drained and wearied, he tossed his cell on the bedside table and was finally able to fall into a deep and dreamless sleep.

CHAPTER 10
INVESTIGATIONS IN NYC

The call from Ethan was upsetting. McKenzie missed him greatly and knew the break-in would be terrible for him. In the space of only a few months, she had grown remarkably close to this man and being with him just felt right to her. She closed her eyes and remembered the fall evening they had sat together in the yard swing at her house and watched the moon.

They held hands and his were warm and strong. She felt his fingers, long and straight with nails cut short and blunt. Practical, that's the word to describe Ethan, she thought. He was a common-sense practical man who seemed to exude goodness. His body was warm next to hers, and she leaned her head on his shoulder. The smells of night surrounded them; dew-damp grass, sleeping flowers, and clean air.

It was a beautiful and quiet moment for the two of them now only a few months after they had met, and for her, it seemed to epitomize the reasons she loved being back in Minnesota.

However, New York was where she was now, and she needed to gather her thoughts about the coming meeting with Detective Garcia.

It wasn't easy as thoughts of Ethan and his dilemma kept sneaking in her mind, as well as lingering guilt over the kiss with Michael. She was seeing a side of Michael she'd never seen before and was struggling with doubts about whether he had really changed that much from their long-term and simpler relationship from before she moved to Deep Lake. She and Michael had sex in those years, yes, but it seemed to be more about passion than about caring. She knew he strayed, but it was almost as though it was expected in their world, and it really hadn't bothered her all that much. She was busy with her workdays, and evenings with Michael were always exciting and glamorous. They went to the theatre often, and special restaurants where it was important to be "seen," and many business-related dinners. Quiet evenings at her place or his were rare. He seemed different now, and his words of caring were more than unusual. The kiss they shared the evening before was fueled by a different sort of passion that she'd never before seen in Michael. She blushed as she remembered how caught up in it she had become.

She was standing at her window steeped in thought when someone coughed quietly. She spun around quickly to see Detective Garcia standing in her doorway.

"You may not have been a million miles away, but it was a long way for sure."

Embarrassed, she admitted, "You're right, I was in a world called confusion, if I have to be honest. Come in, please, and help me get back to this one."

Entering and sitting in her guest chair as she sat in hers, he hesitantly began, "I hate to do it. You looked like you were pondering much more pleasant things than what I have to tell you. I don't want to spoil your illusions."

"Illusions. That's awfully close to delusions, and I'm afraid that's what I was thinking about just now, Detective. What can I do for you this morning?"

"Call me Garcia, please McKenzie. We should be on a first-name basis by now, and I have some news that may surprise you. At least, I hope it's surprising and not shocking."

"Shocking?"

"Yes. I'd like you to come with me on a little field trip, if you will, away from your building."

"A field trip?"

"That's right. We're going to see someone I know, and we might end up somewhere for lunch afterwards, if that works for you."

"My schedule is yours, Garcia, that's why I'm here." McKenzie was thinking she was glad she wore low shoes that day and perhaps the "field trip" might involve some walking.

McKenzie told Gayle they were leaving and would be back later, and she and Detective Garcia left the building.

They picked up coffees and walked the few blocks to Central Park. Garcia had told her he wanted to talk privately, so they chose a bench to sit on. McKenzie had learned there were more than 9,000 such benches in the park, and most of them were adopted by individuals. The one they chose had a small plaque saying, "Meet me here, Lew, you know I still love you." McKenzie would have loved to know the story of how the bench got inscribed, of course, but that was a thought for another day.

Garcia began as soon as they sat down. "I wanted to talk frankly with you away from your office. We've completed the final results for the autopsy on the girl found in Suite 2D. First, she had more heroin in her body than anyone might have injected in themselves. Someone else injected her—and the result was almost instant death. She had many injection sites on her body, and most of them were in places she couldn't have reached by herself. Someone was keeping this girl quiet for a long time. At the end, that someone definitely used enough of the drug to quiet her permanently."

McKenzie drew in a nervous breath and shook her head. "How terrible for her. I'm not naïve, Detective, but this does shock me. Why would anyone do this to another human being?"

"In short, for money," he replied curtly. "Money makes the world go 'round, they say, and it's sadly true. A friend of mine is joining us shortly. She can't afford to have me come to her establishment, and I wanted you to hear from someone who knows how things go in the sort of situation we believe the girl in 2D might have been involved. In fact, here she comes, now."

McKenzie looked up as a middle-aged woman came up to them and shared their bench. The woman was heavily made up and wore a flowing multi-colored dress of a gauzy fabric. Her hair and eyes were black as obsidian. She wore several bracelets that clinked together as she moved her arms, and every finger wore a ring.

"McKenzie Ward, meet Jewels LaRue."

"I'm glad to meet you, Jewels. You live up to your name, your jewelry is stunning."

"It's all part of the trade, sweetie."

Garcia interrupted, "Jewels is the madam of 'Jewels' House of Jewels,' which is, as I expect you can guess, a house of prostitution behind the façade of a jewelry shop. She runs a tight house with clean girls, and cooperates with me when I am pursuing issues like the one we're currently working on."

Jewels broke in, "I can't stand it when young girls are forced into the business, especially when there are plenty who choose the career. The world's oldest profession is an honorable one when everyone involved understands their role. Those sons of bitches who traffic in innocent young girls make me sick! I…"

Garcia continued, "That's what makes Jewels valuable to me because we do understand each other and the roles we play."

McKenzie looked back and forth between the two in surprise but refrained from asking questions.

"The second thing we found in the girl's autopsy was that she was likely from one of the small Central American countries. She had been branded in a way that we have discovered identifies the trafficked girls. We're still working on deciphering the brands for specific countries."

"Branded?" McKenzie blurted while her stomach lurched.

"Yes. We believe this girl was one who was lured or captured from her country and illegally transferred to New York and burned with a brand to recognize where she came from. The girls are sold for prostitution. All madams and the pimps who work with them are not so forthright or incensed by this practice as Jewels is."

"That's for damn sure," Jewels started. "Those assholes…well, I have to cover up my collusion with people like Garcia here, so I have bought a couple of the girls. They arrive in the saddest shape you can think of, having been drugged for weeks sometimes, and they seldom adjust to the real world again. I try to set them free after they've made some friends and I think they can get on by themselves. It takes a long time, and there's no guarantee. They have so much to learn, and the bastards who bring them here don't care about them at all."

"That'll do, Jewels. In fact, that's all I need from you today. You can go back to work and thank you again for doing what you can to keep your business on the up and up."

He covertly handed her what must have been folded up money, and before walking quickly away, she looked at McKenzie and said, "Stay as sweet as you are, dearie, the world's a hard place."

McKenzie watched her walk away and Garcia looked around carefully to be sure she wasn't being followed.

Seemingly satisfied, he went on, "I thought you'd be more inclined to believe me if you met Jewels. She's truly a gem and has helped our department several times with abducted and trafficked girls."

"Coming from where I've been living for the past year, it's hard to believe this sort of thing goes on. It's all so sad."

"Sad, yes, and brutal. And it isn't confined to New York. This stuff happens everywhere, and I expect if you looked around a little more, you'll find it happens in Minnesota, too."

McKenzie sighed and nodded slowly in reluctant agreement. She had done some checking online and recently discovered that sex-trafficking most certainly did exist in Minnesota. In fact, at one time, Minneapolis was one of the top locations in the U.S. for child sex trafficking. A six-month study by local prosecutors found over 34,000 advertisements posted online for sex in the Twin Cities.

"We've looked into the possibilities of the girl we found in 2D and believe she might have been one of a group of young girls who were brought here to be sold. Who's behind the operation is what we don't know yet. We have some prospects and are looking hard at the Ward Building."

"That's frightening. I see now why you wanted me to come back here. Am I one of your prospects?" she asked in simple honesty.

"You were. I have to say that I didn't trust you in the beginning, but now that I've interacted with you a little more, and saw how you related to Jewels, I'm hoping that the shock at what you're learning might help with more information about who might be behind the business of importing girls."

"Wow. This is getting even scarier. What is it you want me to do? How can I help?"

"We need a focused eye on what goes on in your building. You're the perfect one to casually walk the halls and watch for anything that might be odd. Have conversations with the people you meet, check out the basement parking areas for unexpected vehicles and that sort of thing."

"I could do that. I really don't have a job to do here other than be available to you and your department to get this awful business solved. Anything else?"

"This will help you get reacquainted with your tenants, and you can look for people who shouldn't be there. People who don't have a business reason to be in the building; people oddly dressed or nervous, or who won't look you in the eye. It's hard to be more specific, but do you get my meaning?"

"I think so. I've always been curious and people-watching is fun."

"This may not be fun, McKenzie. It could be dangerous if you're not careful. I'll be only a phone call away, so put me on speed dial and let me know of anything you see that strikes you as not being quite right. It's a lot to ask of you, but you are in the perfect position, and now that I'm getting to know you a little, you are the perfect person to do this, without raising suspicion with others in the building. No one else, absolutely no one, can know what you're doing. Are you okay with all of this?"

"It sounds a little scary, now that you get into the details, but I love sleuthing, and this is something I'm good at. I'll do it."

With a satisfied grin, Garcia shook her hand. "You're on. The food vendors are out, the smells have surely improved in the past hour. Have you had a street cart dog yet?"

"Not yet."

"I'm buying and there's a good guy nearby. What kinda soda?"

"Sprite. And a dog with everything."

He loped off to get their food, and McKenzie relaxed on the bench. The park was getting busier close to lunchtime, and office workers were spilling out of buildings to find their favorites from vendors or restaurants. She thought more about what she had agreed to do, and while it made her a little nervous, she was determined to help with the investigation. The death of the young woman in her building was something she could not accept or tolerate. She missed Otis and decided to call him later for any advice he could give her about clandestine people-watching.

Garcia came back laden with loaded hotdogs, chips, and their drinks. They spread the food out on the bench and settled down to a delightful lunch. Biting into her dog brought back memories of hundreds of lunchtime dashes for just such fare. She closed her eyes after her first bite and groaned, "Mmmmm, that's good!"

Garcia grinned again and said, "Hey, you really are a New Yorker. Welcome back!"

CHAPTER 11
SURPRISING ARREST IN DEEP LAKE

Assistant Sheriff Otis Jorgensen was at his desk in Deep Lake and had just hung up with Sheriff Gary Walker. His head was bent and he rubbed his eyes in worry. The conversation had not gone well.

Otis had sat down in his office moments before taking the sheriff's call, coming in early after a wonderful breakfast of blueberry pancakes with Mary Jo and the boys. The small building that housed his Deep Lake office had once been a shed at the side of one of the town's oldest homes. The county purchased it and the small piece of land around it in the 1950s to be used as a makeshift office and meeting room for the county sheriff. The building sat near the carriage house of the main house which had been made into a popular bed and breakfast. The little building morphed through the years and now featured a small conference room, two holding cells, a counter and desk for a deputy and Otis's no-frills office. His furniture was vintage 1980s rejects from other county offices, plus some post-Korean war metal file cabinets and hardwood chairs. His own chair, however, swiveled and had arms plus a soft seat that was formed to his own. He sighed as he settled into it.

Suddenly, the phone rang insistently. How a phone could ring insistently was something he never had considered, but he felt a serious sense of dread when he picked it up.

"Otis Jorgensen here."

"Otis, Gary. We've got trouble. A body has been found in St. Paul. A syringe was near the body and it's got Ethan Thompson's prints all over it. I'll be there in an hour, and you'd better have Thompson in custody."

Otis swallowed the bile that erupted in his throat, and mumbled into the phone, "Yeah, I'll bring him in."

After a few minutes of trying to compose himself, Otis reluctantly called Ethan to see where he was.

"Hey Ethan, where are you now?"

Startled, Ethan answered, "Well, good morning to you, too, Otis. I'm still at home. I can't do anything at the office so I'm just hanging out at home right now after I called some more long-term clients to tell them we're temporarily out of business."

"Stay there, I'll be right over," Otis replied bluntly, and hung up.

With dread leaking out of every pore along with nervous sweat, he headed for Ethan's house in his squad car.

On the way, Otis was wishing that McKenzie could be there with Ethan. He knew this would not be good.

◆◆◆◆◆

Ethan was standing in his front yard, coffee cup in hand. He was dressed in a simple plaid flannel shirt and jeans, and the Red Wing heavy boots he wore when doing farm visits for big animals.

Otis pulled into the driveway, got out of his car, walked over to Ethan, and shook his hand while they greeted each other. He craved this moment of closeness and he feared it might be his last with his good friend for a long time.

Ethan questioned, "What's going on Otis? You sounded so serious on the phone."

"It is serious, my friend. We've got trouble. Big trouble. I've been told to bring you to the station right away. I'm not arresting you, but Sheriff Walker wants to talk with you."

"You're not arresting me? For what? Otis, what's going on?"

"I can't tell you, Ethan. You just have to come with me, now."

With wide eyes and a questioning look, Ethan quietly got in the car when Otis opened the door, and they drove to the station in silence.

Sheriff Walker was already there when they pulled in. He walked out to meet them as they got out of Otis's car, and immediately said gruffly, "Ethan Thompson, you're under arrest for the murder of Buddy Kraus." He continued and gave Ethan the Miranda Warning while putting handcuffs on him: "You have the right to remain silent. Anything you say can and will be used against you in a court of law. You have the right to speak to an attorney, and to have an attorney present during any questioning. If you cannot afford a lawyer, one will be provided for you at government expense."

Ethan was completely dumbfounded by the whole procedure and meekly allowed himself to be led into the station for questioning. He shook his head at the statement about needing an attorney and said, "I haven't done anything wrong, why would I need an attorney?"

CHAPTER 12
AGONY IN DEEP LAKE

Otis had one other person in his office, Lieutenant Lloyd Strother, who helped with investigations and arrests. Lloyd had thoughtfully made coffee for all of them and brought it to the meeting room.

Sheriff Walker had commandeered the building's meeting room and ordered Ethan to sit across from himself and Otis at the room's conference table. It was immediately turned into an interrogation accommodation, and silence followed as they all realized the gravity of the situation.

Ethan clutched his coffee cup as though it was a lifeline to sanity in an insane situation. He was confused, scared, and anxious about what was happening, and hearing that Buddy Kraus was found dead was terrifying. He looked at Otis for a glimpse of hope, but Otis shook his head slightly and looked down at the table. Friendship had to be set aside and both of them knew at the same time how devastating it was going to be.

Sheriff Walker started the questioning. "How did you know Buddy Kraus?"

Ethan answered slowly, "We went to the same high school in Fond du Lac, Wisconsin. We were both on the hockey team there for three years."

"You were seen manhandling Buddy Kraus in Joe's café. You can't deny it because a number of people saw you grab him and say something that witnesses said sounded threatening."

Otis broke in and said, "We all know this type of behavior isn't normal for you, Ethan. Tell us what caused you to grab Kraus in Joe's place and what happened to make this guy end up dead."

Ethan took a deep breath and began to tell about the hockey team and the end-of-the-year "party" at the barn. When he got to the part about the screaming horse, he lost control of his emotions and tears came. "I tried and tried, but I couldn't save that old horse. The fire was getting worse and the other guys pulled me out of there just in time as it turned out. The whole barn caved in and the horse stopped screaming." Ethan closed his eyes and all of them were quiet for a few moments.

He continued, "We all knew Buddy started that fire. We didn't know if it was on purpose or an accident, but he started that fire and none of us ever talked about it. The whole thing was ruled an accident, and because it was the end of the school year and graduation was coming up, it was all hushed up and nothing was ever done about it. The farmer said the barn was falling down and the horse was old and ready to die soon anyway. I think he was an uncle of one of the guys or something and nobody was ever charged or anything in the incident. Summer came then and we all had jobs or college or other plans and we never got together again."

Walker asked, "How did you get reconnected with Kraus?"

"I never saw him again until he walked into Joe's while I was having lunch last week."

"Why did he look you up?"

"He wanted money. Things didn't go well for him through the years and for some reason he decided I might be an easy mark, I guess. He showed me some pictures he had taken during the fire at the barn. He had a disposable camera that none of the rest of us knew about and he used it to capture the rest of us in compromising ways. Of course, he wasn't in any of the pictures and nobody even knew he was snapping them."

Otis couldn't help himself and blurted out the obvious, "He was going to blackmail you!?"

"Exactly. I was furious at his saying he would go to the police with the pictures if I didn't pay him what he wanted. I couldn't have that. That's when I got so upset I stood up and grabbed him. I don't even remember what I said, but that's what people saw."

"What did he do then?"

"He just laughed it off and left. I sat there a few minutes; then paid my bill and left."

Ethan continued, "And that's the last I saw of him. I don't know where he went or if he was staying anywhere in town or anything. He just left, and I didn't see him again."

"You didn't see him again?" Sheriff Walker questioned.

"No, I haven't seen him at all since that day in Joe's."

The sheriff added, "His body was found in St. Paul early last night behind the Days Inn near 94 and I35. He had been injected with Etorphine, a large animal sedative that is up to 3,000 times more potent than morphine."

Ethan gasped, "I use that drug, but it's only for really big animals. I have some farmers with huge draft horses that sometimes get massive muscle damage and they need to be sedated."

Walker continued, "Yes, we believe the drug came from your clinic, Ethan. The syringe was found and the only prints on it are yours."

Ethan hung his head and put his hands over his face.

Walker went on, "This blackmail story clinches it for me, Thompson. You had the motive, the means with your clinic and access to drugs, and the opportunity with plenty of time on your hands with the clinic closed and wrecked. All that certainly adds up to probable cause."

He went on, fueled by new thoughts, "I think you smashed up the clinic by yourself. You needed an alibi for the loss of drugs, and you decided to take this guy out of your life for good."

Ethan shook his head dismally and looked at Otis. "You know I didn't do this, Otis. You've got to help me here!"

Heartsick, Otis couldn't look Ethan in the eye. His mind was whirling with what Walker had surmised, and things looked even more grim than he had feared.

Walker stood up and announced, "Ethan Thompson, you're already under arrest in suspicion of the murder of Buddy Kraus. I've read you your rights and you will now be taken into custody and held in the Washington County jail in Stillwater until your arraignment for this crime."

Without time for Ethan or Otis to think fully about what was happening, the sheriff then pulled Ethan to a standing position, put his hands behind his back and closed handcuffs on him with a loud click.

Walker looked at Otis and reminded him to turn off the recorder of their entire conversation and walked Ethan out to his sheriff's car. He opened the back door, held Ethan's head with a warning to be careful, and sat him behind the screen. He then shut the rear door that had no working handle from inside, giving him no way to get out. Within moments Sheriff Walker drove off and Otis was left to stare hopelessly after his captive friend.

CHAPTER 13
NYC GOOD NEWS AND BAD NEWS

McKenzie woke to pelting rain on her bedroom window. It was the first rain she had seen since being back in New York, and she opened the window to smell and feel the air's freshness. Sidewalks around her building were steaming from cool water against heated concrete, and the rising mist quieted the morning sounds of the city. The smell of summer garbage was dulled and the air assumed a savored odor of clean for a small moment in time.

Taking in a deep breath, she acutely missed the tranquility she had found in Deep Lake where the air smelled fresh all the time, and in the spring smelled like freshly mowed grass.

She hadn't been able to catch Ethan on her call to him that morning and left a message wishing him a good day. She knew how upset he was about the clinic break-in and was sure that his whole week would be taken up by dealing with the aftermath of getting the place cleaned up and finding out who had done the damage.

Her heart was hurting for Ethan and she wished she could be with him to soften the blow of the trashed vet clinic. However, as it was working out her role in the death of the woman in 2D seemed to be getting more and more essential to find the perpetrator or perpetrators. After all, Otis was there with Ethan, and his clinic assistant, Ginny, would be a big help in cleaning things up. She convinced herself that he would be fine without her.

She dressed in a taupe-colored pant suit for the day with low-heeled shoes, expecting to be doing some walking around the building as she greeted her tenants. She felt a little guilty about her reasons for the walk-around and the idea of spying on them for the police didn't sit well. However, she knew it was necessary and wanted to do the best she could to bring both closure to the young girl's death, and help in the hopeful capture of the malicious perpetrators. With a final look in the mirror, she added a bright scarf to her outfit to lift her outlook on the day.

She took the elevator down to the Ward Building office so she could let Gayle know she would be seeing tenants that day. Gayle was her usual cheerful self and said she hadn't seen Desirée yet that morning, but she had a couple of good croissants and coffee for the two of them that they enjoyed in McKenzie's office while Gayle kept an ear for the phone.

"Things are really different here without you, McKenzie," Gayle said wistfully. "We're bigger and busier, yes, but now with you here again, I've been thinking about our times together when you first started this business."

"It seems like a long time ago, doesn't it?" McKenzie was wistful, too.

"We've had some crazy tenants through the years, that's for sure," Gayle laughed and McKenzie grinned.

Gayle remembered, "How about that couple who started a Ponzi scheme from their rented space."

"OMG, that's right! We had some dealings with the police that time, too. Good thing they were found out before they got too many of our other tenants to 'invest' in their ploy."

"That's for sure—I was tempted myself until I realized it was just too good to be true. That's when you started doing a little more investigating into what they were doing and got the police after them."

"I guess you're right. I seem to have investigating in my bones, as a friend once told me. Anyway, I could never have done this business without you, Gayle. You seemed to know which papers I needed at the right time, and if it was a wrong tenant in your opinion, you couldn't find the papers and glared at me a few times."

"And I was right, too!" Gayle emphasized with a palm slapped on the desk and a smirk. "You're a class act, McKenzie Ward, and we needed good and classy tenants in your building. I think I helped with that through the years."

They both laughed at Gayle's forthrightness. "How is it now, Gayle? Do you still have much to say about the tenants?" McKenzie gently probed.

With a sigh, she said, "Not as much. Desirée does most of that herself now, and I have to say we do stay fully leased. We have two new guys who help with paperwork so most of that doesn't fall on me anymore. I can't say I miss it, but now that I'm thinking about the 'old days,' we did seem to have a lot more fun when we were starting out."

They smiled in remembered good times as they finished their coffee.

"Time to start the day, and I think you've got a busy one scheduled, McKenzie."

"Thanks for the breakfast and the chat. You're a special friend, Gayle, and I'll always remember that."

Desirée had called to say she was having breakfast with a potential tenant for 2D when the police were ready to release the space. She was hoping it would be soon. Gayle took the cups away and they shared another smile as they parted.

McKenzie started on her rounds to visit with the tenants, beginning with the florist shop on ground floor. She planned to have lunch with Bernie Williams, the doorman, and Tony Wosika, the building's maintenance man, and hoped they didn't mind that she'd be pumping them for information.

Walking toward the flower shop, she noticed the painting they had done soon before she had left New York the year before. Hallways were bright and clean with a new color called greige that was current but still on the warm side and made the building feel comfortable, and McKenzie liked the mild color. Each tenant had painted their space with colors that appealed to them and worked with their businesses. The flower shop was decorated in bright primary colors with lots of green that made a beautiful background for the flowers. The owner, Sara Hutton, greeted McKenzie in a friendly way and they chatted about Hutton's experiences in leasing her space and working with Desirée's management of the building.

McKenzie remembered Hutton's familiarity with Michael Romano and the disaster of the vibrant-colored flowers he had left in her apartment when she arrived. Thinking about Michael and the strange way he had been acting since she first got back, she wondered how well he knew Sara Hutton. Sara was young and beautiful and certainly fit the type of woman Michael had fallen for in the past. She decided to just be upfront and ask.

"So, Sara, I noticed you seem to be on a first-name basis with Michael Romano. Is he a close friend of yours?"

Sara was nonplussed by the question and actually flushed slightly. "Oh, not that close. He orders flowers now and then, and we talk some. He sees others in the building on occasion so I see him go in and out of here fairly often."

From Sara's reaction, it was obvious that she would like to see more of Michael, but she apparently wasn't yet one of his conquests. McKenzie thanked her for her time and wished her well in her business.

McKenzie's thoughts reeled. Was Michael slipping? Here was a beautiful woman he interacted with frequently and he hadn't even made a pass at her. Could it possibly be that he was sincere about his feelings for McKenzie herself, and his disclosures about love since she arrived were real? This was something she had never expected and now was curious enough to find out more. More thought was definitely needed on this subject.

From the flower shop, she found Bernie who was delighted with her invitation for lunch. They agreed to meet at the building's restaurant, Patisserie Alain, at one o'clock.

McKenzie continued on her rounds of tenants, the financial advisor, and the law office that she noted was larger than it used to be and had taken over another suite next door.

A chic clothing shop had corner windows on second floor and the owner and her assistant tried to be helpful. Unfortunately, they seemed to be kept so busy by the shop that had been there for several years, they didn't watch anything around them very much. Business was good and they liked their space and weren't aware of any problems with the building or management. Good to hear, but not useful for her current objective.

Late in the afternoon, after speaking with many of her tenants as well as after her lunch with Bernie, McKenzie went up to her apartment to think. She made herself a cup of herbal tea and sank into her comfy couch while people and conversations whirled in her mind.

Her cellphone interrupted deep thoughts and she answered with a curt "Hello," without looking at caller ID.

"Well, hello to you, too. Are things that bad out there?" her long-time friend admonished in a smart-alecky pitch.

"Janice, how good to hear from you! I was a million miles away in my thoughts just now and you pulled me back to where I needed to be."

"Now that sounds better. I wondered what happened to my friend and if aliens had abducted you or what."

"I haven't been abducted, but I'm working with the police here on a strange case of someone who really might have been abducted and I'm afraid I'm getting too involved in the whole thing. It's really a mess."

"Oh boy, it sounds like you're back in the detective business. I'm glad I'm not there because I expect that I'd be getting in trouble right along with you."

"You're probably right," McKenzie laughed. Both of them were remembering when McKenzie had been doing some sleuthing for a death that had happened in Deep Lake. She convinced Janice to go with her and the two of them had ended up in a sleezy St. Paul bar with results that were scarily close to catastrophic.

"Kenzie, have you heard from Ethan lately?" Janice asked out of the blue.

"No, I haven't, actually. I've left a couple of messages and texts but he hasn't returned them or called me. I'm planning to try again tonight. I expect he's busy with trying to clean up the mess from the break-in at his clinic."

"I'm afraid it's more than that," Janice said with ominous overtones.

Trouble in Deep Lake ♦ 79

McKenzie sat up in alarm. "What's going on there? Tell me what you know!"

"Slow down, girl. I think you'd better call Otis as soon as you can, cuz he can tell you more than I can. I thought you might have known already and I wanted to let you know I was thinking about you."

"Known what already!?"

"When I was driving to my shop earlier today, I went by Otis's office and saw Ethan in handcuffs and Sheriff Walter put him into his Washington County Sheriff's car."

"What?!"

"I haven't called Otis yet because I thought he might be trying to get ahold of you. I've had a crazy day with a shop full of women and haven't been able to get a break till now."

"Oh, my God, Janice, what's going on?" McKenzie was quickly becoming frantic and paced the floor with heavy steps, overwhelmed by the unthinkable. Ethan was hauled away in handcuffs!

CHAPTER 14

BAD NEWS FROM DEEP LAKE

Troubled and anxious, Janice Hopkins knew something was really wrong when she drove by the Washington County Sheriff's extension office in Deep Lake late that morning. Seeing Ethan Thompson in handcuffs and put into the sheriff's car was a shock. However, she had a full day at her beauty shop and no one there so much as mentioned what had happened. It obviously had not yet been noted by the town's gossips. If anyone knew what had happened, it would be customers of her shop, and no matter how many slight hints she gave, nobody mentioned seeing Ethan in handcuffs. She most assuredly didn't tell anyone what she had seen.

Making the call to McKenzie was scary; either she knew already what happened, or she didn't. Being the bearer of bad news was not what Janice wanted to do, but she had to be sure that McKenzie was aware of what happened to her boyfriend/fiancé or whatever they had become over the past many months.

She and McKenzie had shared many hours together when reconnecting the previous summer after many years apart. Janice, daughter of the only Black family in Deep Lake when they were young, was thrilled to reestablish their high school friendship after such a long time. They had had some good times remembering, and Janice had been a great support in helping Otis and McKenzie in solving some weird crimes that happened in their small town.

On the phone with McKenzie now, Janice tried to calm her down. "Okay, girl. Where are you now; in your office or at home or where?"

"I'm in my apartment. Please tell me what happened to Ethan!"

"First, I want you to sit down. This isn't good news and I don't want you fainting or anything."

"Come on, Janice, you know I don't faint," but just in case, McKenzie sank down onto her soft couch. Closing her eyes, she asked, "Now, please tell me what's happened."

"I don't have the whole picture and as soon as we hang up, you call Otis to get more details. He knows exactly what's up. What I do know is that from what I've learned, a dead man was found yesterday somewhere in St. Paul. It has something to do with the break-in at Ethan's vet clinic, but I don't know what. This morning when I was driving by Otis's office on my way to work, I saw Ethan being put into the back seat of Sheriff Walker's car, and he had handcuffs behind his back. And that's all I know. The rest you'll have to get from Otis, and I thought you might have already gotten the news."

McKenzie was silent for a moment while absorbing this shocking summary. "Oh Janice, this can't be true! Ethan is the kindest, most wonderful…I don't know what to think. I've been doing some information-gathering for the detective I'm working with on the murder that happened in my building, and I didn't have my cell on for most of the day," McKenzie said softly. "What's happening with Ethan, Janice? We all know he couldn't have done anything wrong!"

"We hope not from the man we know. But we don't have the details—we can't know what's going on until we talk with Otis. Will you call him now?"

"As soon as you get off the line, my friend. Thank you for letting me know there's trouble."

"Of course, that's what friends are for. I'm here when you need me, so call no matter what time it is. Neither of us is likely to get much sleep anyway."

"Hmph," was all McKenzie was able to answer.

"Later," they both said at once, and hung up.

◆◆◆◆◆

No sooner did McKenzie cut off the call with Janice, than she hit speed dial for Otis Jorgensen. She was shocked and appalled that she hadn't listened to her messages or kept her phone on all day, but she had no reason to expect bad news, and she was extremely wrapped up in the young girl's murder in her building.

Otis answered after the second ring. "Kenzie, I've been trying to reach you."

"I know, I just talked with Janice and she knows something is up. What's happening there, Otis?"

"Did Janice say anything about the gals in the beauty shop spreading rumors?"

"No, she said nobody knows what happened this morning with Ethan, and she kept it quiet."

"That's about the only good news I've had today," Otis took a deep breath. "Things are not good here. Ethan really needs you back here. Any chance you can get away?"

"I don't think so, Otis. I'm working with a detective here on a terrible murder in my building and it's really my responsibility to help him for a few more days, anyway. Tell me what happened!"

"It's a really long story. You know about the break-in at the vet clinic, right?"

"Of course. Did you find out who did it yet?"

"Sheriff Walker thinks Ethan did it himself."

"No way; he wouldn't do such a thing. He loves that clinic!"

"Yes, way. A man Ethan knew from many years ago was found dead. He had been given a shot of a powerful large-animal dose of anesthetic. The syringe came from Ethan's clinic and had his fingerprints all over it."

"Otis, that can't be true!" McKenzie screamed, as she jumped up and began to pace the room.

"You can't imagine how much I want it to be not true, Kenzie, but facts are facts. You know I'm not supposed to be sharing any of this with you, right?"

"Absolutely. But we've done this before, remember. It helps you to talk it out and I've got a good ear. But this, this is almost more than I can deal with," and McKenzie's tears started to flow.

Otis didn't know how to handle tears, so he ignored them. "Turns out this dead guy was somebody Ethan knew from high school back in Fond du Lac, Wisconsin. He was threatening to blackmail Ethan for something that happened with their hockey team back in high school. That's why Sheriff Walker is so convinced that Ethan did it."

"Otis, what can I do?"

"Nothing. You stay where you are and just come home as soon as you can. I feel as bad as you can guess, and I'll do whatever I can to get Ethan out of this mess. I do have some ideas I'm working on, but right now things are not looking good for him."

She groaned. "Where is Isabella with all this going on?"

"She's with her grandma in Edina, and you know she'll take good care of her."

"She will. Can I talk with Ethan at all?"

"No, not yet. He will be arraigned tomorrow and I'm not sure what will happen then. He's in the county jail for now and this is premeditated murder they're talking about, so I don't even know if he'll get bail."

"Oh, Otis. How did things get this bad? We know Ethan is a good man. He *couldn't* do this!"

"I don't think so either, Kenzie, but we have to follow the rules for now. I'm working on this full-time and my deputy will manage things at the office. I think all you can do right now is pray, and you know I mean that."

McKenzie was sniffling with more built-up tears, and she almost dropped the phone. "Thank you, Otis for all you're doing. *Please* get him out of there," she whispered frantically.

"I'll do what I can, and you know it. Hang on and pray and I'll call you when I know any more."

Chapter 15
Janice Goes to NYC

McKenzie stumbled to her bedroom and collapsed on her bed, sobbing. How could life get so out of hand and frightening?

She knew Otis was a knowledgeable and efficient law officer and she had no doubt that he would get to the bottom of what had happened. He said he had some leads and would start following up on them right away. Maybe he was right that all she could do now was to pray. She determined to do that non-stop, thinking about her wonderful Ethan locked in a tiny cell in the county jail. Oh, dear God, how could he survive in there? Her pillow was soaked with tears and she sobbed even more until exhausted, she finally fell asleep.

◆◆◆◆◆

Morning came with clouds and misty rain and McKenzie woke with a headache from crying. She looked in the mirror at her swollen face and eyes with bags like purple plums. A glance out the window led her to mumble that even the day was crying.

She pulled on sweats and an old hat and joined the herd of damp and sour people running in the park, but her heart wasn't in it. She missed her faithful Goldie running by her side; she missed her house; she missed familiar streets and other early risers she always waved to; and she missed Ethan badly.

Even a shower didn't perk her up as it usually did, but she plodded through getting dressed for the day. She had more tenants to see and try to get information from—and it was time to start. Instead, she sat in her tiny kitchen with coffee made from her single-cup pot…and prayed. Otis was right. That was the only positive thing she could think of to do.

Her cell jangled beside her, and this time she did look at the ID. Grabbing it like a lifeline, she let out her held breath as she whispered, "Janice."

"I'm coming. I'm on a late afternoon flight that gets in about six. I've already got a ride; no need to pick me up at LaGuardia. Believe it or not, I called and pretended like I'm the country hick I really am, and got an UberX right to your building."

"How did you manage all this? You've got a shop to run! I can't take you away from your mom and all you have to do."

"Mom is fine on her own for a few days, and I own the shop, remember. Vicky is thrilled to look after it all for me, and she sends her love. Look for me about seven-thirty, eight o'clock, or whenever the traffic allows, and I'll be hungry, so all you have to do is feed me. A bed would be good, too."

"You are a godsend, girl! Food I'll get, and your room will be ready—you can bunk at my place. Thank you from my heart. I can't wait to see you!"

Janice, McKenzie's strange and wonderful friend from typing class in high school. Strange because she didn't talk to anyone in school, much less blond and blue-eyed McKenzie, and wonderful because they struck up an unlikely bond, in a hostile way at first, in typing class. They competed from then on in every way possible, and Janice usually won whatever it was except for the really academic stuff. For example, hair. Janice had a huge Afro in high school because it was popular then. McKenzie had flat, stringy blond hair that she just blew out of her eyes most of the time. Janice's mother had a way with hair and she created beautiful styles that complemented Janice's height and made her look gorgeous every day. One day out of pity she offered to cut McKenzie's hair. That kindness changed her look forever. Mrs. Hopkins also pepped up McKenzie's color and kept her haircuts attractive and easy to care for. They became real friends after that, but lost touch when McKenzie went away to college and her eventual success.

The girls connected again after McKenzie returned to Deep Lake the summer before, after seventeen years in New York, and realized they still cared about each other. In fact, they seemed to have even more in common and became closer friends as adults. Janice by then owned her own beauty shop and was doing well with her life. She hadn't married either but was a beautiful chic dresser and a stunning presence with her slim six-foot height.

Janice and McKenzie had done some sleuthing together when Otis was investigating a murder in their town the last summer, and they got into a bad scrape. Fortunately, they were rescued by Otis, and it brought them even closer.

McKenzie rallied from the good news that her friend was coming to help. She finished fixing her face as good as it was going to get and dashed down to her office.

After filling Gayle in on who she'd be seeing that day, she immediately got busy with her tenant visits in eager anticipation of seeing Janice later. She was hopeful that together, they would be able to ferret out what information was needed to help the police solve this crime as quickly as possible. As much as she wanted to jump immediately on a plane and go to Ethan, she understood that her ownership and long-term knowledge of the building was needed by the authorities. She also believed that Janice's presence would help her concentrate on getting the right information from the tenants. She was committed to helping Garcia and his department to find who was behind the murder of the young girl, and then she could finally get back to Deep Lake where Ethan needed her to be.

CHAPTER 16
ARRAIGNMENT IN DEEP LAKE

Breakfast at Otis and Mary Jo's house was hectic what with getting the boys ready for school amid the two rambunctious goldens that were wagging their hairy tails and licking everyone and everything within reach. Mary Jo was trying to make pancakes and shared her "mistakes" with the dogs who replied with happy lapping.

Otis said, "I'm beginning to know why I go to the office so early lately," rubbing Ben's head in affection.

"Oh, Dad," Ben replied, "it's so fun with Goldie here. Honey really likes her. I miss Isabella now. She would really like to play with Honey and Goldie after school. Is she ever coming home again?"

"Of course she is, son. She's staying with her grandma for a while until her dad…uh…"

Albert interrupted, "I heard somebody at school say Isabella's dad killed somebody, Dad. Is it true?"

Otis and Mary Jo shared a worried look. He took a deep breath and tried to reassure them all. "The sheriff and I and the whole department are trying to get to the bottom of things, Albert. We can't make any judgements until we know everything that happened. First of all, Ethan is our friend, and we can't forget that."

Ben piped up, "He helped Goldie's feet get all better when she got hurt that time, remember?" Otis surely did remember because that was how Ethan and McKenzie had met almost a year before. The dog's feet had been viciously slashed with broken glass, and Ethan had to first rule out McKenzie's involvement in what had happened. He then worked with both McKenzie and Otis to find out who really did it.

"That he did, and he's a great dad to Isabella. If you hear anyone talking about it at school, you can say that nobody knows what happened yet and the sheriff's department is working on finding out. That should be enough to stop the gossip."

Albert answered, "I hope so. I really like Doctor Thompson."

Mary Jo said, "So do we all. We hope this mess can be cleared up soon and we can get back to normal life. We're missing Kenzie, too and hope she will be back home before long. Now, off to school with you two, and to work for Dad. It's time for the hairy ones to play in the back yard a while so I can get some work done here."

Kisses and hugs were exchanged, the door slammed several times, and Mary Jo collapsed at the kitchen table with her second cup of coffee. She then put her head in her hands and prayed out loud. "Dear God, please bring a peaceful end to this business with Ethan and bring Kenzie home. I'm so afraid of what might happen when people lose their way. Amen."

◆◆◆◆◆

Otis first went to his office and was reassured his deputy, Lloyd, could handle things for the day unless something major came up, so he headed for Stillwater.

As expected, Ethan Thompson was brought before the Washington County Court and arraigned for murder in the first degree, plus lesser charges of destroying his own veterinary clinic and using drugs therein to murder Ronald D. Kraus aka Buddy Kraus.

Ethan's lawyer was a criminal defense attorney named Mahalia Abbott-Kennedy. She was a seasoned, gray-haired bi-racial woman from Minneapolis, and known for sticking to the rules. She was tough, but fair in all of her dealings, according to Oliver Freeman, lawyer husband of McKenzie's work friend, Tracey.

The judge was a slightly younger former colleague of McKenzie's father, Judge James Archer Ward, Jr. The Honorable Robert C. Calaway was also a rule-follower and fair in his dealings. He was only a few years from retirement and was curious about this case involving his former friend's young veterinary friend.

Mahalia Abbott-Kennedy had tried her best to convince the judge of Ethan's reliability when meeting with him out of court before the hearing, because Ethan didn't want her to attend the arraignment.

Ethan was dressed in a suit and tie and a dark blue shirt, clothes brought from his home by Mary Jo Jorgensen, because his parents, uninformed at this point, were back in Wisconsin. He was pale and looked sort of absent. His hair stuck out in odd spikes like it hadn't been combed, and his whole demeanor was like he wasn't really there.

Mary Jo sat in the courtroom along with Otis and Sheriff Walker, as the county prosecutor formally stated the charges against Ethan. When asked his plea, Ethan whispered "not guilty" in a small voice.

Judge Calaway acknowledged the seriousness of the crime and everything about it. However, no matter how reliable he was said to be according to Abbott-Kennedy, he ordered Ethan to be held in the county jail without bail for the foreseeable future or until the trial. The gravity of the crime was devastatingly brought home to everyone involved.

Everything was over after only fifteen minutes. Ethan was led out of the courtroom in handcuffs by two guards and his shuffling feet that never cleared the floor made the only sound.

Disbelieving and still in a state of shock, Sheriff Walker, Otis, and Mary Jo quietly left the room as well.

Outside, Mary Jo shook her head sadly at Otis and got into her car. The sheriff and Otis talked briefly and the sheriff left.

It was going to be a hard spring.

CHAPTER 17
FRIENDS CONNECT IN NYC

When McKenzie's first few interviews with her tenants were ineffective, she realized how upset she was. She decided to put off any further contacts until Janice was there to accompany her the next day. Instead, she went to lunch with Gayle. They had been close friends through the early years as McKenzie's business took off, and Gayle was a big part of that success.

Both were pleased that it was just the two of them and they got a great private table at Patisserie Alain. They caught up a little more with what each of them had done for the previous year since they'd seen each other. They had a lot to talk about and chatted easily over fabulous French pastries. However, as time went on, McKenzie began to sense that Gayle wasn't all that happy to be working with Desirée. She decided to ask her specifically what had changed.

"Gayle, I feel that something is different in the office these days. I know that Desirée has made some changes and she has certainly brought more business our way. How do you feel about all of that? Are you okay with the changes?"

Gayle's eyes widened. "I wasn't going to go into all that with you; you've got enough on your plate right now."

"That's part of what's on my plate, and I think it's time to cut into it."

"Well, as long as we're being honest here, I don't know if you're aware of how much Desirée herself has changed since you left."

"Changed—how?"

"Some of our clients aren't up to the standards that you expected and we stuck to for so many years. Some of them come and go too quickly, and their businesses are suspect from my view. I guess my trust has been a little shaken by some things she's done."

"For example?"

"There's a massage parlor in 3C that I wouldn't have leased to and I know you wouldn't either. It seemed at first to be on the up and up, but it's getting more traffic than I would expect for such a business. Desirée handles everything for that business by herself and none of the rest of us has gone near it. When it comes to competency, I don't like the looks of the young woman who runs it at all."

"Whoa—that is specific. I need to check this out, and soon."

McKenzie told Gayle about Janice's arrival that evening, and that she would be helping to interview some of the building's residents in view of the young girl's death. "You can help me a lot by making a list of the businesses and people you might have suspicions about. You still have files on each of the tenants, I expect, and have been saving any bits and pieces of information on them, right?"

"That I do, and I'll look for flags on all of them."

"Janice and I will check out your list tomorrow and see if we can come up with anything that might interest Detective Garcia. Does that work for you?"

"It sure does. Desirée has changed a lot over the past year, and not for the good. I've been wanting to tell you about this, but I was reluctant to bother you."

"Bother me? Absolutely not! This could be a big help to solve the murder, and besides, I need to know about Desirée's behaviors. Something just doesn't smell right about this whole thing. Thanks for your help and for being candid with me. We'll talk more tomorrow after you get me your list. I'm eager to see it."

"Thanks, McKenzie, I feel better already," Gayle said with a sigh as they left the restaurant and went separate ways.

McKenzie took the afternoon off and did a little shopping at the greengrocer and deli just down the street to get ready for Janice's visit. They'd go out, of course, but it would be nice to stay in and visit for some of the time as well as to share what they might find out about the tenants. McKenzie was getting more and more eager to see her friend.

♦♦♦♦♦

At seven-thirty on the dot, McKenzie's phone startled her out of thought. It was Janice. "I'm at your front door, girl, and the doorman asked if I wanted 3C."

"Aha—we'll be checking that out first thing tomorrow. Have him send you up to 8A where I'll meet you at the elevator. Your wine is already poured."

"At last!"

Moments after the elevator door opened, the two girls hugged and cried, then laughed and hugged and cried some more.

In McKenzie's apartment, after stashing Janice's bag in the guest bedroom, they sat at the kitchen table sharing news and catching up. Otis had taken Janice to the airport and on the way filled her in about the arraignment hearing at the courthouse. There was nothing anyone could do at that point, and more tears were shed as Janice shared the news. They drank wine and nibbled on the deli goodies bought that day and drank more wine. It wasn't long before both of them changed into their PJs and they sat on the floor by the fireplace. Janice had some good ideas about helping with the interviews, and they strategized about how they would do them the next day.

In all, it was a wonderful reunion with so much happening over such a short time. At midnight, Janice said, "If we're going to kick ass tomorrow, I've gotta get some sleep, Kenzie, and so do you."

"You got that right. We're gonna kick ass all over this town if we have to, to figure this thing out. Hey, girl, I'm so glad you're here." They hugged again and shuffled off to their beds.

CHAPTER 18
ETHAN SUFFERS IN DEEP LAKE

Otis walked with Mary Jo and the sheriff outside from the courtroom. In contrast to everyone's mood the day was beautiful, with sunshine and early spring hopes of green grass and flowers all around, and tree buds ready to burst. When the others left, he turned toward the county jail hoping to get permission to talk with Ethan. He *needed* to hear from Ethan's mouth what had caused this horrible mess. What he had told McKenzie was totally false. He had no clues, no leads to follow up, no evidence whatsoever that might clear Ethan's name. At this point, he didn't even know where to start.

Otis felt as though he had been whipped after the arraignment hearing, short as it was. He was confused, scared for his friend, and sick with worry that there might be even a remote possibility that Ethan really did kill Buddy Kraus.

After some time and paperwork, he was finally able to get permission to see his friend. While doing that, he also discovered Ethan had refused to see his attorney, Mahalia Abbott-Kennedy, who tried to see him just minutes before Otis tried. The whole situation was disastrous.

Ethan agreed to see him, and Otis made the dreaded trip to the jail. No matter how many times he had been to jails or prisons as part of his occupation, he never got over the frightening feeling of being locked down deep in the heart of an unforgiving building behind barred doorways. He was ushered through clanging gates and along the way was stripped of anything that might be construed as dangerous, even his shoelaces. He finally entered a room through a heavy metal door that was guarded inside and out by stone-faced sentinels with eyes like slate.

Ethan was seated at a scarred wooden table with narrow deeply scratched benches on either side. His head hung low and touched the prayerful hands folded beneath his chin. He was dressed in an orange jumpsuit that hung on him like rags on a scarecrow. On his feet were scuffs, with no laces.

He looked up as Otis sat down across from him and tears began coursing down his cheeks. "Help me, please. You know I didn't do this."

Otis took a huge gulp and began to talk with his friend. "I want to help you, Ethan, but you've got to be honest with me. Your actions so far have only seemed to amplify your guilt and I don't know how to do it. My first question is why did you not want your attorney with you at the hearing? She's supposed to be good and Judge Ward's and McKenzie's friends have gone to bat for you already by finding her."

"But I didn't do anything! I didn't think I needed an attorney and I thought if I had one it would look like I was guilty, and I'm not, Otis, I'm not!"

"Oh hell. Let's start at the beginning. Tell me how you knew this Buddy guy and how this all got started."

Through quiet questioning, Otis was able to lead Ethan through the barn-burning and the death of the old horse, and Buddy's suspected part in causing the debacle. He also told him about seeing Buddy in Joe's recently, and the blackmailing threat. He insisted that he had not seen Buddy at all after that unfortunate confrontation. He also insisted that he had no knowledge of how his clinic had been invaded and looted. He was just as dumbfounded as everyone else on that front. As far as killing Buddy Kraus, it was all a total surprise to him.

From the expressions on his face as he told the story, and the innocence in his eyes, it was apparent to Otis that this was a set-up by someone else. How to find who did it was a problem, and the problem was getting bigger.

♦♦♦♦♦

The next day, Otis started by making a list of people identified by Ethan's recitation the day before. He planned to interview people like Timmy, the boy with Down syndrome who worked at Joe's. According to Ethan, Timmy had seen the whole confrontation between Buddy and Ethan. He might have a different point of view from others, and of course, he wanted to interview others in the restaurant, too.

He wanted to talk with Ginny Sherwood, Ethan's clinic helper to establish what sort of relationship the two of them had, and if she had boyfriends who might be jealous or curious about the drugs she watched over. He needed to contact suppliers of the drugs kept on the premises to see if their records tallied with Ethan's account.

In addition to all that, he wanted to contact some people from the high school in Fond du Lac to see what they remembered. He didn't want to drive all the way to Wisconsin, but would do it if necessary. Did Buddy have a wife, and if so, where was she and what did she know?

The list was getting longer and longer. At least he had a place to start and a few ideas to begin the process. He wished McKenzie was there to urge him on and to provide the little side comments that seemed to help so much in miniscule ways, but always grew. It was time to call her with an update such as it was. He knew she had to be waiting anxiously to hear from him.

♦♦♦♦♦

"Otis, I've been waiting for your call!" McKenzie picked up the phone lying beside her plate of scrambled eggs and toast. Janice nodded silently. The two of them were sharing a quiet breakfast as they strategized the morning's visitations.

Otis filled her in on the arraignment hearing and Ethan's refusing the attorney. He also told her briefly about the long-ago barn-burning and seeing Buddy turn up in Deep Lake at Joe's with blackmailing language.

"He has to use that attorney; she was highly recommended by Oliver Freeman as well as my dad's former attorney, and it sounds like he's going to need the best representation he can get."

"You got that right. Kenzie, this is looking bad for Ethan. Now that I've got his story, I really know he didn't do it, but proving it is gonna be tough. I'll do the best I can and will start on some interviews today. The sheriff isn't convinced, so that could be a problem. You gotta get back here soon; he really needs you."

"Janice is here and we're gonna tackle this murder thing together. I have problems here, too, but we'll get them fixed. I'll get back there as soon as I possibly can. You know that's where my heart is already. Take care of him for me, Otis, I need him, too!"

♦♦♦♦♦

After the call with McKenzie, Otis made a few more calls and started his investigation with renewed focus.

His first visit was to Joe's Café.

CHAPTER 19
QUESTIONABLE MASSAGE IN NYC

Immediately following McKenzie and Janice's breakfast, Detective Garcia called. He wanted to know if any headway had been made on tenants and if McKenzie needed help with the interviews. She was happy to tell him that Janice had arrived and would help her with the tenants. He didn't know Janice, of course, and was a little suspect of her abilities. McKenzie grinned to herself and thought, "wait till he meets her…" They made arrangements for a late lunch with the three of them to share results and thoughts about the interviews and how the case was progressing.

Janice was dressed in a total power look and wore a deep purple silk suit by Anne Klein with a short tight skirt. Her hair was piled high, and she tottered on matching four-inch heels. Overall, with her six-foot height, she was an impressive presence. McKenzie, in a slightly understated navy skirt-suit, looked at Janice and just said, "Wow!"

They shared a nervous laugh and split up to check out the Ward Building tenants because they didn't want the people to feel ganged-up-on. Janice took some of the older tenants and McKenzie headed directly to 3C, the massage parlor about which Gayle had suspicions.

◆◆◆◆◆

McKenzie walked through the clear glass door of Missy's Massage and was immediately enveloped in sounds and scents. Looking around at tropical island posters on the walls, it was apparent the sounds were waves lapping gently onto a beautiful island beach that might be real, or it might not. Scents included tropical flowers and palm trees mixed with the smell of an ocean breeze. Missy herself, a beautiful young Asian woman, was at the counter, with a flower in her shining black hair and dressed in a colorful sarong that matched the posters. McKenzie introduced herself as the owner of the building.

"Oh, Miss McKenzie, I'm so happy to meet you. I thought that Miss Desirée was the owner of this beautiful building, but she told me you were here and might be stopping by."

"Did she now," McKenzie replied. "I have been wanting to meet my new tenants and see what sort of businesses you're running. Would you mind giving me a short tour of your facilities? I hope this isn't a bad time."

"Oh no, this time is good. We have four treatment rooms at this facility and only two are busy at the moment." She led McKenzie through a hallway painted in soothing ocean colors and opened the door to a treatment room. The large spa treatment table took up most of the room, with cabinets around the perimeter. McKenzie took the liberty of opening a cabinet door to expose the contents, including oils, stones, various electronic products, a myriad of sprays, lotions, and more. Piles of cloud-white towels took up another cabinet. Another small room held a tanning bed, and all looked appropriate for the business as it was supposed to be.

McKenzie quizzed Missy a little more. "Are you the owner of this business?"

"Oh, yes, Miss McKenzie. I have a spa license."

"How long have you owned it?"

"Almost a year now."

"How did you start your business? I mean, did you work somewhere else first, and how did you get the money to start this business?"

Missy began to look a little nervous. She was very young, but a spa-owner certificate could be earned in as little as six weeks, McKenzie knew. However, getting the capital and knowhow to run a business as successful as this one appeared to be, was another thing. McKenzie kept questioning. "Did someone help you with your business plan before you started?"

Missy's eyes began to shift around. She said, "I work in another massage spa before I come here. I don't know about a business plan."

"Who is your business partner, someone who helps you do marketing and planning?"

"I don't know about business partner, but when I have a question, I call Miss Desirée and she tell me what to do."

"Miss Desirée."

"Yes, she very helpful," and Missy nodded and smiled.

"How many other people work in the spa?"

"Varies. Sometimes three girls, sometimes more if many clients, and Mr. Aki." At this, she actually giggled.

"Who is with the people in the two rooms here that you told me were getting treatments?"

"Miss Ming is with man in Room 1; he have body massage. Mr. Aki is in Room 2 with lady who get hot stones."

All was most interesting and seemed to be on the up and up, however, the competence of Missy as a business owner was surely questionable and McKenzie was eager to follow up with Desirée to see what her involvement was. Disturbing as well as most interesting overall.

McKenzie decided that was enough questioning until she talked with her own "business partner." She also wanted to talk with Detective Garcia to see what his reaction was from speaking with Missy's Massage. Something was definitely off in that corner of the building.

Catching up later with Janice, she heard she had interviewed three other businesses while McKenzie had been in 3C. In addition, Janice had made an appointment for a shampoo in the beauty salon for after lunch, knowing from experience that was the place to go to find out anything.

Turning her phone back on, McKenzie found she had missed three calls from Michael. He wanted to take the girls to dinner that evening. McKenzie wanted to ask Janice what she thought about dinner and decided lunch in the park would be a good place to do that. They could talk about their morning discussions without anyone overhearing and enjoy the outdoors as well.

Janice opted for a cheesy pretzel and McKenzie found a taco in a bag. They grabbed a bench—this one just said "Miriam"—and munched.

Over hot caffe lattes they shared their findings from the morning. Janice agreed that something was really wrong with the massage parlor and little Miss Missy was nothing more than a pawn in somebody's bigger game. Desirée had some explaining to do.

While sitting in the park, McKenzie called Detective Garcia because she was already nervous about confronting Desirée by herself. She wanted to know what he thought about her findings. He agreed to meet the two women at her office right after lunch and was very much interested to hear what she found out.

CHAPTER 20
INTERVIEWING IN DEEP LAKE

Timing was good; Otis went to Joe's about ten-thirty, just after the breakfast rush and before lunch. Most tables were empty and staff was getting ready for the lunch rush. He spoke with Joe, the owner, and the waitress, LaVonne, who had served Ethan on the day of the confrontation.

Joe Rogers was a tall, skinny guy who you'd never guess owned a restaurant, thin as he was. Heavy smoking was a bad habit and he spent a lot of time outside the back kitchen door after non-smoking became the law. Married with five kids, he was a long-time Deep Lake resident, and had owned his family restaurant for twenty-five years or more. All of his kids grew up knowing how to flip burgers and serve customers, but all were off starting their own lives and none had stayed around to take over Joe's when he might be ready to retire. However, when times were lean or extra help was needed, you often saw a Rogers' kid helping Dad on a weekend. Mom did the books for the restaurant at home, but after the kids were gone, she did her part at Joe's, too. It was a good family venture and many teenagers from the town got their first jobs at Joe's.

"You know Ethan Thompson, Joe, this business has to bother you, too. Tell me what happened when he is said to have grabbed this guy from out of town," Otis began.

"Of course, I know Doc, comes in here all the time. I never saw him do something like that ever. Doc is a really nice guy. I happened to be at the cash register at the time, and I had a clear shot when Doc jumped up and grabbed this guy by his shirtfront. I heard Doc say something real quiet and then it got louder, but I couldn't actually hear the words they said. He let go of the guy and the guy said something back and then he left. We were all watching the Doc then, and he sort of shook his hands out like he was shaking off something that smelled bad and he threw some money on the table and he left, too. Timmy cleaned off the table later and he said Doc didn't even eat his lunch."

"And that was it?"

"Yup. I never saw the guy again and I didn't see Doc either. Then we heard about the clinic getting broke into and Doc got arrested. That was a surprise, I'll tell you—nobody expected that to happen. What's gonna happen now?"

"Good question, Joe. We've got a ways to go to get it all figured out, but we're working on it. Thanks for your help, and call me if you think about anything else or hear any scuttlebutt that might be going around."

"Will do, Otis. You said you wanted to talk with LaVonne, too. She's right over there and has time now."

LaVonne, a long-time server and also a resident of Deep Lake, was glad to get off her feet for a few minutes and talk with Otis. She wore the brown and tan uniform like others in the restaurant and filled it out a little more than some. She remembered the event well. She had tried to get an order from the stranger, but he said he didn't want anything. As she was walking away, she saw him eating fries off Ethan's plate. She had come back after a few minutes and was only a few tables away when Ethan jumped up and grabbed the guy, and she heard him say something that sounded mean.

"Mean? Tell me more about that," Otis said.

"Well, Doc sort of whispered something really hard and it sounded mean to me. That's why I looked at them, it was so unusual for Doc to talk like that."

"And then?"

"The guy sort of laughed it off and said something really loud, like 'See you later,' and he walked out of the restaurant. That's the last I saw of either of them. Then I heard the man was killed and Doc has been arrested for it. Is that true, Otis?"

"I'm afraid it is, LaVonne, I'm afraid it is."

Otis then saw Timmy cleaning up tables and with permission from Joe, he sat down with Otis. He was nervous, though, and said, "Don't sit here—for customers."

Otis tried to assure him that it was okay to sit in a booth with him for just that day, but made a note that if he had to talk with Timmy or others from the restaurant further, it would be at the station.

Timmy had worked at Joe's for several years busing and cleaning tables, and it was obvious he loved the work and took great pride in what he did. Joe called him his best employee, and Timmy made sure Otis knew it. Otis first asked Timmy his whole name, which was Timothy Peterson, each syllable drawn out slowly. Before Otis could say anything, Timmy also added, "Used to be different, but that's my name."

Otis went on, "Yes, now you're Timmy. Your mother, Linda Peterson, works at the Deep Lake Bank?"

"Yes, she likes the bank. Makes money to take care of me."

"And that's a good thing, right, Timmy?"

"Yup," he said with a grin.

Otis decided he might as well be blunt and get right to the point. "Remember the day that Doc Thompson grabbed a stranger when he was here for lunch?"

"Sure do. Doc is nice to me but he was mean to that man. The man ate Doc's fries. Doc likes fries."

"Have you seen that man before, Timmy?"

"No. He made Doc mad. Don't want to see him."

"Yes, Timmy, I think you're right. He was a bad man. Anything else you want me to know about the man or about Doc when they talked together?"

"I want Doc to be nice to me. I won't eat his fries."

"Thank you, Timmy, if I need anything more, I know where to find you. Keep working hard and I hope you stay Joe's best employee."

"Yup, me, too!"

Otis got a coffee to go and went back to his station to think. Ethan's clinic assistant, Ginny Sherwood, was due in his office shortly. What would she be able to add, he wondered.

CHAPTER 21
DISCOVERY IN NYC

Back in her office, McKenzie asked Gayle to get a message to Desirée to meet with Janice and herself at two o'clock. She told Gayle that Detective Garcia was also coming, but to not mention it to Desirée.

Garcia was arriving at one-thirty, which would give them time to share information before Desirée joined them.

At one-twenty-nine, Garcia knocked on McKenzie's office door. Janice opened the door to him and the look on his face was almost comical. As he took in her astounding appearance and had to look up to meet her eyes, he was speechless. McKenzie saved the day and introduced her longtime friend, "Detective Garcia, my friend and co-faux investigator, Janice Hopkins, from Minnesota. Janice is discreet and I trust her confidently with any of the information on this murder case."

He cleared his throat and said, "Welcome to New York, Ms. Hopkins."

After an uncomfortable moment of looking at each other, particularly Garcia and Janice, McKenzie directed them all to sit because there was information to share. She started. "Garcia, Janice has been helping me interview our building tenants and we are curious about some responses."

"That's great, McKenzie, I was hoping you would have some questions. Let me first catch you up on what we've found out so far, if that's okay with you."

"That would be great," McKenzie said and both she and Janice nodded.

"The great news is that we've discovered who the dead girl is. Her name is Teresa Pinedo and she's from El Salvador."

"Teresa," McKenzie whispered and closed her eyes.

"We got lucky with her DNA and found a match to her brother in the city of Acajutla, El Salvador. The brother is not a good guy and his DNA was in the system for a rape he was convicted of about a year ago."

"We believe she was kidnapped by someone who might have known her brother, and she was hidden on a cruise ship at first."

"Wow," McKenzie breathed. "What a brother."

Janice interrupted, "Detective Garcia, we have to tell you that we're under a tight timeline this afternoon. We've got some information that might incriminate someone from this office and she is joining us in twenty minutes."

Garcia looked up and raised his eyebrows, inviting more. "Tell me what you found."

McKenzie continued. "Janice has a hair appointment later today in the salon on third and we hope to get something there, also. However, I spoke with Missy Vang from the massage spa this morning, and I was impressed with how little she knows about running a business. Supposedly she is the owner of the spa, but she referred to my business partner, Desirée Canard as knowing a lot more about the business and the one who answers questions for her."

"Aha, I'm glad you got to her. When we interviewed the tenants previously, Missy was not available, and I spoke with a Mr. Aki. He was pretty convincing that the business was legit, but I had doubts and was hoping to catch her. What else did you find out?"

McKenzie continued, "It's very suspect in my opinion. This girl knows next to nothing about business of any kind, and in my mind, she's a pawn for somebody."

"Mine, too," Janice agreed. "Desirée Canard is coming here at two to talk with us about what we found out."

"Good work, both of you," Garcia said. "If you don't mind, I'll take the lead in talking with her today. I have to tell you that we've had suspicions about Desirée and were getting close to asking her about several questionable things."

McKenzie and Janice looked at each other and nodded. "That's okay with us," McKenzie said. "This is really bothering me—I want to hear how she answers."

At two o'clock, a knock came at McKenzie's door, and Desirée walked in. She was startled to see Janice and Garcia there, and together the four of them crowded the room. McKenzie introduced Janice to her and found her a chair. McKenzie also said they were called together to talk about information gained from tenant interviews and Garcia would continue from there.

Desirée interrupted and said impatiently, "Those interviews were done days ago—I thought you were looking elsewhere for suspects for this stupid drug killing. It's obvious the girl was doing drugs and her pimp or a "customer" killed her. New York City has almost half-a-dozen deaths a *day* from drugs. Can't you clear this up so we can get back to work? I've got a client on the hook for that space and he's getting anxious."

Garcia stood and paced by the windows. "You're right, we do need to get this killing cleared up. We did do the interviews several days ago but we're still finding new information that needs to be checked out. For example, Desirée, tell us a little more about Missy's Massage in 3C. We finally were able to talk with Missy Vang, the registered owner of the business, and we have some questions that I believe only you can answer."

"You talked with Missy? I thought you already spoke with Mr. Aki, the manager."

"We did speak with Mr. Aki, at your request, I might add, however we finally found Missy just this morning and had an enlightening conversation with her."

"I see," Desirée mumbled and looked down.

"Let's stop beating around the bush, Ms. Canard. Exactly who owns Missy's Massage? It obviously isn't Missy."

Desirée sighed and in a quiet voice, said, "I do."

McKenzie blurted out, "*You* do? Desirée, you know this isn't ethical and is against our policies, don't you?"

"Yes, I know. I'm sorry, McKenzie, but I needed money, and this seemed so easy, so foolproof, I couldn't say no."

Garcia interrupted, "I think that's enough for now, everyone. Ms. Canard is going to come with me to the station so we can talk more about who this person she couldn't say no to might be."

They all stood, Desirée looking like a million in a designer silk suit, but now her head was hanging in embarrassment. McKenzie silently shook her head as Garcia led Desirée out the door. He nodded at Janice and McKenzie and said, "See you later."

CHAPTER 22
INTERVIEWS CONTINUE IN DEEP LAKE

Ethan was still in the county jail. He had finally taken Otis's advice and agreed to speak with his attorney. Abbott-Kennedy reported to Otis later that Ethan was extremely depressed and was hardly eating. He did, however, answer all her questions and tell her about the barn-burning so long ago. He told her that Buddy Kraus had mentioned having photos of everyone but himself at the fire, but he didn't show Ethan any photos. He had no idea where they might be.

What was known to attorney Mahalia but not to Ethan or most obviously to his would-be blackmailer, the statute of limitations for the state of Wisconsin where the barn-burning and the death of the horse had occurred, was six years for felonies. Their crime was not a felony, and most likely was considered a misdemeanor which had a limitation of three years, so no additional charges or penalties would apply twenty-some years after the deed was done. In fact, the actions of the authorities involved at the time indicated that the whole event was determined to be an accident and no charges were ever brought against the young men then or ever would be.

This information should have been known by Ethan and anyone with a modicum of education, but his own personal guilt over the death of the horse was so strong, he wasn't able to think clearly about that issue.

Mahalia decided Ethan wasn't in a comfortable place in his mind at that point to fully grasp all the implications of the statute of limitations, so she didn't yet tell him about it.

She did remind Otis of it when they spoke after her visit with Ethan. Otis replied, "Yes, I know what you're saying. None of us were aware of what Ethan was worried about, and we need to tell him this when he's in a little better shape to understand and accept it. I will be calling the authorities in Fond du Lac to verify the information and see if they are aware of Kraus's attempt at blackmail for the fire. I'll see if anyone from there has any information we could use. Somebody killed this guy—and I don't believe it was Ethan Thompson."

Mahalia agreed, "I don't think so either, but his mind is still so troubled over that incident with the horse dying. He really did believe that Kraus was going to try to blackmail him."

Mahalia left after they both agreed to share any information they found that could impact Ethan's trial that had not yet been set.

◆◆◆◆◆

Mahalia had cornered Otis just as he was going into his office early in the morning. He was planning to interview Ginny Sherwood, Ethan's clinic assistant who was due at the station in less than a half-hour. Thankfully, Lloyd had already made a big pot of coffee. Otis poured himself a fresh cup and sat down in his conference room to rearrange his thoughts and think up some questions for Ginny. No sooner had he sat down, than Ginny came knocking at the door. The only thing Otis Jorgensen disliked more than people who were habitually late, was people who liked to arrive early. He needed his prep time and Ginny walked in on the beginning of it. Lloyd wasn't aware that Otis needed more time so he had led her right into the conference room.

Coffee and pleasantries were quickly dealt with and she and Otis sat across from each other. Otis learned that Ginny was young, eighteen, clear-eyed, and blond like so many others with her Scandinavian background. She had graduated from Stillwater High School the year before at seventeen and was working to earn money before going to college. Her dream was to become a veterinarian like Ethan, but her family had several other children and couldn't afford the costs for college at that time. She was patient and knew she'd achieve her goals and as she said, she had a wonderful mentor in Ethan.

Her respect for her employer was openly noticeable, and she teared up when Otis told her he was in the county jail until his trial for murder in the first degree. "I just don't believe he could do such a thing, Mr. Jorgensen. It all has to be a terrible mistake."

"Do you have a boyfriend, Ginny?"

"Yes, I do," she sniffled.

"Tell me about him; is he a student, does he work, how long have you known him—that sort of thing."

"Well, I go out with Johnny Iverson. He graduated with me last year and he goes to Century College now. He lives at home with his parents and they are neighbors to McKenzie Ward, Ethan's girlfriend. I've been dating Johnny for about six months or so. He was a little wild in high school; used to play in a band with a bunch of guys, but now that he's in college, I like him better."

"How about drugs or alcohol. Do you and Johnny like to party?"

She blushed and picked at the collar of her plaid blouse. "We have a beer sometimes if we're with others. I don't believe in drugs, and Johnny doesn't either."

"Come on, not even weed?"

She blushed even more. "Johnny gets some sometimes, and I tried it once. I didn't like it and I told him I won't do it again."

"What does Johnny think of your job with Doc Thompson?"

"He's cool about it. I told him I'm learning a lot and he thinks that's good so I can be a vet someday."

"Did you and Johnny break in and wreck the vet clinic on the night of April seventh?"

Ginny put her hands against her mouth and her eyes almost popped out of her head. She screamed, "No! I'd never do anything to hurt Ethan's clinic. I love my job there and I don't know what to do with myself until I can go back. How can you ask me that?"

"What about Johnny? You have keys to the clinic; did he ever ask you about getting drugs from there or suggest you might go there to party sometime?"

The girl was crying hard by this time. She scrabbled in her purse for tissues but gave up and her shirt front was already wet. "I would never do that, and Johnny would never ask me to. We just wouldn't. Yes, we party sometimes, but it's always at somebody's house or in the woods. We're not like that!" She was sobbing and her nose was running and mascara was streaking down her cheeks.

If this was an act, she was good at it, Otis thought. That was enough and he reached for tissues for her. He said, "I'm sorry if I've upset you, Ginny, but we need to find out the truth about what happened that night and the next when Buddy Kraus was murdered. Someone did these terrible deeds and we have to find out who it was."

Ginny silently nodded.

More gently, he asked, "Do you have any other information that might help us?"

She shook her head.

"If you remember anything—any little thing at all no matter how small, please call me right away, okay?"

She nodded and looked at the floor.

"You can go now, but I may have to talk with you again. You can tell Johnny what we talked about, and maybe together you can remember something that might help us. Thank you for coming in and please believe me that we're doing everything we possibly can to figure all this out."

Ginny nodded again and slowly walked out the door.

◆◆◆◆◆

Otis sat down again and shook his head. He was getting nowhere with this case, and the longer it took him to shake the branches with little falling out to look at, let alone investigate, the longer Ethan would have to sit in jail. And, as much as it pained him to think about it, the guiltier Ethan looked.

CHAPTER 23
SHOCK IN NYC

McKenzie and Janice were shocked when Desirée Canard admitted that she actually owned the massage spa in the building. This raised all sorts of questions in their minds as well as Detective Garcia's, and when he took her to his station for further questioning, they were even more shocked.

McKenzie watched Garcia leave with Desirée, and she just said, "Whew, now what?"

Janice said, "Remember I still have an appointment at the beauty shop, and I've got to run to get there on time."

"Yes, do go—who knows what more information you might find out. I should have done that days ago but didn't even think about it. We'll talk about dinner when you get back."

McKenzie stood in the middle of the room and was thinking about whether she should continue interviewing her tenants, when she turned her phone back on. It beeped immediately with a number of messages, and then rang with a call from Michael.

"McKenzie, I've been trying to reach you all day. Have you just been busy or what? You're beginning to worry me."

Instantly deciding to keep the information about Desirée to herself, she replied, "Everything's fine, Michael, just busy, yes. My friend Janice from Minnesota has come to stay with me for a few days and we've been busy."

"Janice, is she the one who has a beauty shop there?"

"Yes, that's the one. She's a good friend."

"Well, how about I take the two of you for dinner tonight? I've missed you while you've been working with this detective to figure out the murder of that girl in your building. Anything new on that front?"

"Nothing really new on the murder mystery. I've talked with the detective and they are pretty stumped at this point. Dinner would be good, but I'll check with Janice and get back to you about what sort of food. Okay with you?"

"For sure. Call me and I'll make reservations for seven so we can make it an early night for you two. I'm eager to meet your friend but I'm more eager to see you. Later."

McKenzie went to see Gayle at the front desk, who was still stunned that Desirée had left with Detective Garcia, and what was more stunning was that Desirée was not in charge. Instead, Desirée had looked scared when she left with Garcia and Gayle had never seen her like that before.

"Okay, are you going to tell me what happened, or do I have to guess?" Gayle began.

"McKenzie took a deep breath and said, "I'll tell. The problem is there will be more to come, I'm afraid. I don't know how this is all going to play out. The big news is that the massage parlor in 3C is not owned by the young girl who has been posing as the owner. She's just a puppet; Desirée owns it."

"What? Desirée owns it? What's going on?"

"Don't know yet. I hope to hear from Garcia before long. Meanwhile, Janice and I are going to dinner with Michael Romano tonight. There's safety in numbers."

"Numbers?"

"Gayle, Michael has been acting weird ever since I got here. I might be totally wrong, but I just don't trust him like I used to. He's changed. I don't know what it is, but he's not the Michael I used to know. Having

Janice with us for dinner might help to bring out something I'm missing. Know what I mean?"

"I think I do. McKenzie, Michael Romano has been spending more time in this building than he ever did when you were here. It seems that I'm always running into him buying flowers or getting a massage or something. Before, he only came here occasionally to see you. I've wondered, too. What changed?"

"Good point. I don't know yet, but I hope to find out. I didn't tell him about Desirée's going off with the detective. I hope you don't spill the beans about that in case you see him."

"My lips are sealed. I can't wait to hear what she tells the detective. This funny business has to be stopped, and however I can help it happen, you know I'm with you."

"I know, Gayle, and thank you for being on my side for all these years. We'll get it figured out, no doubt!"

♦♦♦♦♦

McKenzie went up to her apartment and before long, Janice came back from the hairdresser. She looked fantastic, which was no surprise, but her hair was gorgeous, with a four-to-six-inch pouf on top of her head and the sides slicked back and smooth as silk.

McKenzie had made some coffee and they sat to talk about the day. She told Janice about dinner and Janice was eager to meet Michael because of all she'd heard about him.

"Is he as gorgeous as I've heard?"

"Even better. Trouble is the old saying of beauty being only skin deep is turning out to be truer than I ever thought. There's something wrong about him since I got back. He's not the same old Michael. He keeps telling me that he loves me and that's something that never came up with us before, even after years of dating. He never would have even said the word. It doesn't feel right to me."

"How can having someone love you be wrong?"

"It's not real. I know love now, real love with Ethan. It's kind and gentle, full of joy and caring. It's compassion, concern, and lovingness toward someone you long to be with. In other words, it's something Michael has no clue about. Oh, Janice, I need to be there with Ethan," she cried. "We *have* to get this thing cleared up so we can go back to Deep Lake and help him!"

Janice opened her arms to her friend and they hugged for a long time. "It's going to happen, girl, it's going to happen."

◆◆◆◆◆

What Janice didn't tell her friend before dinner was that the women in the beauty shop were all crazy about Michael. Every one of them knew him and that he was gorgeous and successful and rich. They saw him often in the Ward Building, but nobody seemed to know his real business there, except they saw him going to the massage parlor quite often, and he regularly came to the nail shop next door for pedicures. They heard the staff fought over who would do his pedicures, because he was a great tipper. It sounded like he had never approached any of them for a date or anything, and he never really talked about anything of substance with any of them while he was there.

There was talk about the massage parlor and the surprising amount of business they did for being a small shop, but no one seemed to suspect foul play going on. They talked about the murder and most believed it was druggies from the outside who somehow got in and left the dying girl in an empty spot. Janice hadn't learned more than she expected but left the door open to trying again.

McKenzie called Michael after she and Janice talked that afternoon. They decided because there were two of them, he wouldn't try anything fishy that night. They asked for Thai food. Michael agreed and said he knew of the perfect place and would pick them up at seven. Both of them kept their tops on they had worn for the day and changed their skirts for pants and lower shoes, thinking they weren't trying to impress anyone for the evening and wanted to be comfortable.

CHAPTER 24
THE PLOT THICKENS IN NYC

At seven o'clock Michael Romano stood outside the Ward Building while the evening doorman ushered out McKenzie and Janice. McKenzie made the introductions between Janice and Michael, and noticed his eyes widen as he realized how tall she was and how good looking, as well.

"Good evening, ladies, how beautiful you both look," he said elegantly. "You didn't tell me your friend was so exquisitely lovely," he said to McKenzie.

"I wanted you to be surprised," she answered. "She has that effect on people," and both women laughed.

"Exquisite or not, I'm hungry," Janice said.

They climbed into a cab with Michael who said the Thai restaurant was nearby and he hadn't taken his car. Restaurants changed quickly and this wasn't a place McKenzie knew about. She noticed him giving Janice a side-eye as they rode, and they made light conversation. He was most definitely fascinated by her.

At the restaurant, they ate delicious Thai food including Spring Rolls, Pad Thai, Pineapple Fried Rice, Pad Kee Mao, and more. Janice was greatly impressed and said, "How can I go home to our little Deep Lake Chinese take-out place ever again?" and they all laughed.

Michael brought up the topic that was burning in each of their minds, "So, how are you coming with your crime busting venture, McKenzie? Any luck?"

The women looked at each other. They had already decided to not tell Michael much if anything of what they learned that day. Instead, they wanted to query him to see what he might know and not be talking about.

McKenzie began with a sigh, "Not so good at this point. Janice came to support me, and I'm really grateful, but I'm hoping she can help to do some sleuthing, too."

"Sleuthing?" Michael asked.

"Well, we did a little investigating together before, but we haven't always had the best of luck," Janice answered.

McKenzie looked at Janice and rolled her eyes and said, "That's not much of a humblebrag the way she tells it."

"What do you hear from the detective on the case?" Michael wanted to know.

The women looked at each other and McKenzie answered, "I think he's going to share some information with us tomorrow. I'm not sure what he's found out."

Michael said, "They may never find out. There's almost half-a-dozen drug deaths a day in New York City, and this looks to be one of them."

McKenzie caught herself from making an audible gasp because he was using the same words and saying the same thing as Desirée had earlier that day, and she knew that Janice had caught it, too. Obviously, Michael and Desirée had talked together very recently. However, they believed it was before she was taken to the station by Garcia, and that was a good thing. They didn't think Michael knew about that.

Michael went on, "The girl probably followed somebody into the building and found the empty office as a place to shoot up. Unfortunately, she just used too much. Let's not let that spoil our evening. I've missed seeing you McKenzie, even for a day, and having your friend with us is an added bonus. Where should we go after dinner?"

Both McKenzie and Janice wanted nothing more than to go home and get in their jammies and talk, but Michael was pressing them.

McKenzie finally said, "Michael, we stayed up late last night yakking and it's been a long day. Please understand that we need to call it a night. Okay?"

He grunted in disappointment.

McKenzie continued with conviction, "We can make it a more festive evening in a couple of days, but for now, it's time to go home," and both women stood.

Michael couldn't do much after that, so he paid the bill and ushered them out to a waiting cab and they all piled in. At the Ward Building, before he could even get out to open the door for them, both women jumped out. McKenzie did kiss him casually on the cheek and said thanks for dinner, but they practically fled into the building and left him standing in confusion.

♦♦♦♦♦

A short time later both Janice and McKenzie were in their PJs and sitting in front of the fireplace sipping brandies.

McKenzie started, "He must have thought we were nuts, running off like that."

"Nuts or not," Janice replied, "I don't care what he thought. McKenzie, this guy is dangerous. Yes, he's the best-looking man-candy I've ever seen, and he's charming to boot, but I know we both caught him using the same words that Desirée used today. They are in cahoots somehow, and we have to let Detective Garcia know that Michael needs to be looked at more carefully. Agree?"

"Absolutely! It's still early, only nine o'clock, do we dare call Garcia?"

"You have his cell number, right?"

"I do someplace."

"Then dig it out and call him. I don't think we should wait until tomorrow."

McKenzie checked her phone and she had already entered Garcia's number. She pressed it and put him on speaker.

"Garcia here."

"Detective Garcia, this is McKenzie Ward. I'm sorry to bother you at home, but it's something we should talk about."

"Don't worry, I'm still at the station. What's up?"

"Janice and I had dinner tonight with Michael Romano. We were talking a little about the case, and both of us heard him use the same statement that Desirée had said earlier today about 'almost half-a-dozen druggies a day die in New York City.' It struck us both that they had to have talked together very recently to use the same line. Do you think that's right?"

"I do. I also think that I need to speak with Mr. Romano again and very soon, because of this and because of something I heard earlier."

"Can you share anything about what happened when you questioned Desirée Canard this afternoon?"

"Not yet, we're still working things out, but do you think Romano went home after you saw him tonight?"

"I don't know. It was still early so he might have gone somewhere for a drink or something. Janice and I wanted to come home early, so we sort of dumped him."

"Don't you worry about it, we'll find him; we do need to talk. You and Janice stay in tonight and be sure to lock your door tight. We'll talk tomorrow."

Both said good night and hung up.

"Whew," McKenzie blew out her breath. "I think Michael would kill me for telling on him like that." She grimaced after using those words, but Janice added, "Why do you think Garcia told you to lock your door tonight?"

"Do you think he might do something to us?"

"Who knows. I think he's in this up to his neck and I sure hope Garcia finds him, and soon!"

Janice convinced McKenzie that a TV movie with popcorn was what they needed to take their minds off what might have or might still be happening. They agreed and Janice looked for a movie while McKenzie made popcorn.

CHAPTER 25
MORE QUESTIONS IN NYC

After an uneventful, but quite sleepless night, McKenzie and Janice decided they might as well continue interviewing the tenants of the Ward Building. They split up and continued their short visits. McKenzie kept her cell phone on hoping to hear from Garcia about the interview with Desiree and the search for Michael.

McKenzie wanted to talk again with Bernie, the doorman, and Tony, the maintenance guy. She made appointments with each of them for late morning to meet in the vacant space of the office at 2D. The crime scene tape had been removed, but the space was not yet released for leasing. She had met there before with Garcia, and presumed she could use it to meet with Bernie and Tony. She wasn't comfortable meeting with them in her office in case Desirée might come in that day.

It was also more than a little creepy for all of them to be where the young girl had died, and might invite more conversation than somewhere else.

Tony Wosika came first. He was a career maintenance man with both plumbing and electric certificates and did a great job of maintaining her building. He had been with the building for at least a dozen years and knew it and its tenants well. Dressed in a clean tan jumpsuit with loops and pockets for the various tools and supplies he carried with him, Tony was a no-nonsense Polish man with a family that lived in Brooklyn. He liked his job at the Ward Building and told her it was because the tenants were of a better class than where he had worked before.

"Yeah, I remember dat furniture guy, Robles, who was in dis space. He got a ton of goods delivered in big crates down in da garage. I hadda help him sometimes and dey was heavy. Hadda put up elevator pads so as not ta scratch da walls. I taught he was a little creepy, sorry Miss Ward, but he was strange. Dem disappearin' in da night like dat…dat was bad."

"Don't worry about that, Tony, tell me about your relationship with Desirée Canard from my office. How do you get along with her?"

"She's okay, but mostly I get my work orders from Gayle in da office, she's great. Don't see Miss Canard much…except she used ta come ta see Robles, here, sometimes. Dunno why, but when I was helping wit deliveries to Robles, she was always hangin' around."

"Interesting. Tell me, do you know Mr. Romero, Michael Romero?"

"Well yeah, he used ta be your boyfriend, before you moved back West, right?"

"You're right, but I'm thinking about other ways Mr. Romero might have been in the building when he wasn't with me."

"Now you ask about 'im, yeah, since you left he been here a lot. He used ta come ta see Robles, too, and I seen him going to da massage place on terd sometimes. Must be nice to have da money to get a massage, huh? Dat place sure gets a lotta business. I never taught men went in for dat stuff, but dey's a lotta 'em dat do."

"Did any of these guys ever give you money? You can tell me, Tony."

"Yeah, Robles gave me tips for helpin' wit da really heavy furniture crates. I never opened 'em, dough. Once I got da boxes or crates in da door, he gave me some money and I left right away. He never wanted me to help wit opening da crates. I taught dat was odd."

"It was odd. Tony, I believe Detective Garcia will want to talk with you again, maybe even later today. Please make time to see him if he asks, okay? You've been really helpful for me and I'm sure you feel as I do, that we need to get this murder business solved."

Tony agreed and told her he would cooperate with anyone who asked. She also asked him to keep their talk private and not talk with anyone except Garcia about what they discussed. He agreed wholeheartedly and they parted.

Wow! was all McKenzie could think. It wasn't looking good for Michael or Desirée right now, especially with their connection with Mr. Robles and his import shop.

She did meet again with Bernie, the doorman, in the empty Robles shop, but she didn't learn much more than they knew already. Bernie was pretty much stuck at the front door all day and didn't see where people went after they came in. However, he did say that Michael was spending more and more time in the building and Bernie was wondering why. He saw him talking with Desirée quite a bit and sometimes she was waiting for him to enter the building.

McKenzie was anxious to hear from Garcia and kept checking to be sure her phone was on.

CHAPTER 26
SURPRISING ARRESTS IN NYC

Keeping themselves busy while waiting for Garcia, McKenzie and Janice made routine calls on other building residents and businesses but didn't find out anything more than they already knew. Janice bought a striking outfit from the India Clothing Boutique, and McKenzie tried on several good-looking pieces, too. The silver shop was especially diverting, and they both found things there.

Finally, McKenzie's phone rang and it was Garcia. He was on his way to meet them in her office. He told her not to worry about Desirée being there because she was already in custody at the police station.

"NO!" she shouted, and other customers of the silver shop started looking. Janice pulled them both out into the hall to finish the call. When Garcia told them Michael was also in custody, McKenzie handed the phone to Janice, because her hands were shaking so violently, she couldn't hold it.

Janice calmly told Garcia they would be waiting for him.

The girls beat it to McKenzie's office, and Gayle asked what was going on. McKenzie told her that Desirée would not be in that day and maybe for a longer period, and that Detective Garcia would be there shortly. At Gayle's wide-eyed expression, she said she would tell her more later, and to please bring three cups of coffee if she had time. Gayle made a fresh pot of her great coffee and Garcia walked in the door.

McKenzie met him and they brought their coffees to her office, shutting the door. Janice was already there and waiting.

Pleasantries were brief, and they all sat down for what could be a long discussion.

Garcia, who looked exhausted with dark rings around his eyes and finger-combed hair, started. "We're winding down. It's taken most of the past twenty-four hours, but Michael has cracked and Desirée has totally fallen apart. I have to thank both of you for confirming your doubts about Romano and sharing information about Desirée. It gave us the break we needed in the case, and it's all coming together."

"Thank God!" McKenzie breathed.

Garcia continued, "We don't have every little detail defined, but it's coming. It started with Mateo Robles and his import/export store here in the building. We're not sure where he came from but he likely had another shop somewhere and left it just as suddenly as he did this one. We haven't found him yet, but I believe it's just a matter of time. We have his fingerprints from some obscure place in 2D, and that's a good beginning.

"Robles was importing large pieces of beautiful furniture mainly from South American countries. What he was also importing was people; mainly young girls who had been smuggled from those countries. El Salvador was a key source of girls, and the victim Teresa lived in the port city of Acajutla. The DNA match for Teresa Pinedo with her brother in El Salvador gave us our biggest break. We know when she was trafficked, but don't know for sure how long the group had been acting before she came to the U.S.

"We believe that Teresa's brother got to know some guys from the cruise ships. They eventually began to trust him and shared what they were doing, which was picking up young local girls and stealing them away to their personal space on the ships. Several of them kept one or two girls locked in their cabins and drugged them to be quiet. When the ships docked in Florida, they were paid for the girls who were whisked away."

McKenzie and Janice looked at each other and both were fighting tears.

"From Florida, the girls were more heavily drugged and sealed in containers loaded with furniture. They were easily hidden beneath or inside the furniture. They had minimal water and a little food, but mainly they slept. The containers were loaded on trucks and sent to various points in the U.S.

"When the containers or truckloads arrived in the garage of the Ward Building, workers were hired to bring them up to Robles' store. The girls were kept in a small room at the rear of the business until they were sold again. On occasion, Robles was seen entering or exiting the building with an exotically dressed young woman, but because of his own South American origin, no notice was taken.

"Teresa was purchased by Robles and came to New York. She might have been one of those 'exotic-looking' women Robles walked out with through the front door when he was delivering a girl to her new owners."

"Purchased!" Janice spit out and shook her head. "It's slavery all over again. I thought that ended with my great-grandparents."

"Sadly, it's still going on in situations like this all over the world. We don't know the full extent of how big this operation is that we're looking at, but we're shutting down some major parts of it and that feels good. The Feds are involved now, and there are likely to be more parts shut down, and some really bad people put away."

McKenzie said, "Tell us more, Garcia, please. How were Michael and Desirée involved?"

"Well, Desirée became friends with Robles and she told us he convinced her there was a great way to make a lot of money that didn't involve much risk. All she had to do was find some businesses that operated in a shadowy-legal way, and the girls would then be sold to those businesses. She would get a 'finder's fee' and be in the clear. She liked that the girls would be taken away and she would never see them again.

"Desirée became friendly with Michael Romano after you left last year. She eventually told Romano about what she was doing. He liked the idea of making money behind closed doors and helped her buy the massage parlor here in the building. He's a silent partner in it and the nail salon next to the beauty shop, too. He managed to bury his interests in the businesses, but his reach goes farther than we know about at this point. We know there is prostitution involved in both ventures and we're working on that.

"Coming down to Teresa Pinedo, she was one of the girls bought and sold into prostitution by Romano. She managed to get away from where she was kept and came back to the Ward Building. Someone found her; we think it might have been Romano himself, and he pumped her full of drugs and left her to die in the empty furniture store."

McKenzie was crying hard by that time, and she could only shake her head. "That poor girl, that poor girl," she said quietly.

"Desirée and Michael have stayed personally involved with each other but they didn't want anyone else to know. He was feigning interest in you, McKenzie, to throw you off the track when you came back. I'm not sure where he expected that to lead, because it sounds like you weren't accepting his attentions."

"I wasn't at all. I knew there was something fake about the whole thing with Michael, but I didn't think it was *this* bad. It's hard to believe how much he changed from the man I knew before." McKenzie shuddered.

Janice said, "You look exhausted, Detective Garcia. Thank you for coming here to tell us what you've learned. You are right that things like this are still happening all over the world, and we have to be diligent and listen to our 'niggles' when we think something doesn't feel right. If it doesn't feel right, it usually *isn't* right and we need to act on those feelings. I'm so glad that McKenzie and I did just that. Things didn't feel right about Desirée and Michael and look what came of it. Whew!"

"You're right, Janice. Thank you for helping McKenzie and being such a good friend."

Garcia tried to hide a huge yawn and stood. Janice took his arm and ushered him to the elevator and McKenzie joined them in the hallway. "You've shared enough with us for one day. Now you need some sleep, no matter how much more there is to do. Our two personal bad guys are behind bars where they need to be, and you've no doubt dealt also with the shops employing the trafficked girls. What a nightmare they went through."

Garcia went on, "This smuggling ring is broad and deep. Our guys are helping the Feds and are following up on all of that. Oh, I should tell you that my friend you met, Jewels LaRue, helped us find another of the trafficked girls who came through Robles and Romero. Jewels has been working undercover for a long time in small ways; this was a big way. Said she liked meeting you, McKenzie, and wishes you a good life."

"Hmmm. You make my staying here seem not so bad the more you talk about it. However, my true home is in Minnesota now, and I can't wait to get back. I have someone there who really needs me."

"Lucky guy. I think we've bothered you enough for now, McKenzie. You and Janice go back home and live your lives. You've both been a great help to the NYCPD, and we won't forget you." With that, Detective Garcia was gone.

CHAPTER 27
MORE DISCUSSIONS IN NYC

McKenzie and Janice were as exhausted as Garcia looked. It was already after six o'clock and the other clerks had left for the day. Gayle was pacing in front of the entry counter and pounced on them the moment they came in after Garcia left.

"Can you tell me now? Please tell me things are going to be okay."

McKenzie asked if there was any wine in the office. Gayle said they kept a few good bottles behind her desk if it was needed. "Now is the time—it's needed—and badly. How about pouring three big glasses and we'll sit in my office. I'll order a pizza—double cheese with everything but anchovies, okay? We've got a lot to talk about."

She and Janice kicked off their shoes and curled up on each end of the couch; Gayle sat in McKenzie's office chair, after toasting to a good future for all of them.

First, McKenzie bluntly asked Gayle, "Are you with me, Gayle? I need to know up front and right away that you haven't been or aren't a part of what Michael and Desirée have been up to for the past year."

"The past year…I'm not really sure what you're asking, McKenzie, but please believe my loyalty is to you. I've been wondering about a lot of things since Michael began spending so much time in this building. I couldn't imagine that as an attorney he would have so much to do here. I thought at first that Desirée disliked him, but things changed recently, and then he began focusing so much attention on you. I've had doubts about him and to be honest, I just don't trust him anymore. I wanted to talk with you about him, but the opportunity didn't come up."

"You still do the main financial work for the building, right?"

"Yes, I always have since you and I worked together from the beginning."

"Have you noticed anything odd or different lately or questionable in your mind?"

Gayle was silent for a time, and then said, "I've been wondering about the massage parlor. Janice, our business tenants' leases are partially based on the traffic of the business and their income and expenses. Mr. Aki brings me the figures for their business, but from the actual number of customers I see going in and out and the numbers on their records, I honestly think there might be another set of books that I don't know about. Now I know that's a serious charge to make, and I'd need to gather more information to really accuse someone of such a thing…"

McKenzie interrupted Gayle, "You're right. Mr. Aki does have a second set of books for that business, and they go to Michael Romano."

"What? What are you saying?"

"That Missy's Massage is owned not by sweet little Missy, but by Desirée, and Michael helps her with illegal management of it. The same goes for the nail salon."

Gayle's face registered shock, "They've been cheating you all this time?"

"That's the small of it all, Gayle. The worst part is that there is prostitution involved and people trafficking, and more. We've been conned, tricked, and deceived, most of all by two of our closest friends. Does this surprise you?"

"Surprise me? I'm having trouble digesting this. In fact…" Gayle ran out of the room to the restroom down the hall and lost her lunch, breakfast, and maybe a few more meals. The shock of hearing about Desirée's duplicity and how trusting she herself had been with her proved to be more than she could handle.

When she came back several minutes later, she carried the pizza that was just delivered. She had paid for it out of petty cash, but her face was still white and she didn't think she could eat anything for a while.

They set the pizza aside, dialed the conversation down a notch, and tried to gently explain to Gayle what had been going on behind the scenes for almost a year. They told about Detective Garcia's involvement in chasing down the myriad details in the case, and the ways that McKenzie and Janice had helped to bring things to a head. Gayle eventually calmed down and they all realized they were starving, so as they were explaining and chatting, they devoured the pizza along with a couple bottles of wine.

It was getting late and they were all winding down into exhaustion. McKenzie offered, "How 'bout we call it a day and get some sleep? This has been a lot to take in and we need to process it individually as we can. Can we meet here tomorrow at say, ten, and try to figure out where we go from here?"

They all agreed and went their separate ways. McKenzie and Janice hardly spoke on their way to their rooms. Inside her apartment, they waved and grinned in a macabre way and went to bed.

♦♦♦♦♦

The next morning over flaky croissants that Janice picked up at the French bakery on street level, they savored their coffee in McKenzie's tiny kitchen.

McKenzie started, "Okay, as far as I'm concerned, this mess is solved. Garcia can handle things from here on and he's working with the Feds now on the larger disaster of the people trafficking. I most certainly hope to never see Desirée or Michael again. I want to go home—so badly I can taste it. Ethan needs me and I need him. I know this man and he's good and kind and could never do the things they are saying he did. If I have to come back here for a trial or something, I can do that in a day trip but I need to be with Ethan."

"That's a good thought, my dear," Janice began, "and I'm all for getting home, too, but you have more to think about than your two-timing friends. Like your business here?"

With a big release of breath, McKenzie said, "Don't I know it," and hung her head. I have some work ahead of me, huh?"

"For sure." She grabbed a small tablet and a pen from the counter and said, "Let's start making some notes on what has to be done before you can get out of here. My round-trip ticket has me leaving the day after tomorrow. Think you can figure things out by then and go with me?"

"I don't know; there's a lot to think about."

"First of all, do you trust Gayle Granville enough to run things for you, and could she do it?"

"I trust her implicitly, and she's way smarter than the work she's been doing for Desirée would make you think. I know she wants to retire in a few years. Maybe she would take things over for a while. I'm thinking of selling the building and the business and everything here, to be honest. It hasn't just been this nasty business that has put a bad taste in my mouth. I'm getting so comfortable in Deep Lake it feels like that's where I belong, and I've been thinking of getting out from under the pressure of this business for longer than you'd believe."

"You're really sure about that?"

"Yes, I am. Now that I've put it in words, it feels even better. Tell me what you think."

"I think you're right on, and you can add fifteen smiley-face emojis after that."

They stood and hugged for a long time and the release of frustration and exhaustion caused them both to get teary-eyed.

"Okay," McKenzie ventured, "Let's get dressed and meet with Gayle and hope she's on board with all of this. That's a big IF but it sure would be great."

◆◆◆◆◆

Pantsuits and comfortable shoes were the order of the day for all three of them. They laughed when they looked at each other when meeting at ten as previously planned. All of them were in some shade of navy and wearing white shirts.

McKenzie asked one of the new clerks to sit at the front desk and answer phones, and she and Janice grabbed Gayle and marched her back to convene in the corner office formerly used by Desirée. It was bigger than the second office with better seating. Additionally, the brighter colors of the room were powerful and the whole scenario was positive and constructive.

McKenzie had also asked the front desk clerk to bring them fresh coffee, which he did willingly.

Comfortably seated and holding their coffees, McKenzie began. "Gayle, I know we shocked you with the revelations yesterday. How are you holding up?"

Gayle smiled, "It was shocking all right. I've done a lot of thinking and putting it all together with my own suspicions that I had tried to bury. I don't know why I didn't figure it all out before. It's hard to think badly of people you know others trust."

Janice broke in, "That's a good way to put it, Gayle. We were talking the other day about paying attention to our 'niggles.' It's important to talk with someone else about things that just don't feel right to you. Often saying something out loud can help to fix what's bothering you."

"You're right. Maybe if I had called you, McKenzie, with my 'niggles,' things might not have gotten to where they are now."

McKenzie replied, "I don't know if we could have stopped any of it. They were in this for a long time and somehow their hearts turned blacker and blacker. Anyway, Gayle, I have a proposition for you."

"A proposition?"

"Yes. I, too, have been thinking a great deal about all of this, as well as my move to Minnesota. I belong there, Gayle, more than I belong here. I hope you can understand that."

"I can. I know you loved your work in New York for many years and you worked hard to build this business. I was proud to work alongside you. But it's obvious to me that your heart is no longer here."

"I didn't think it showed that much, but I'm not surprised. I'm thinking seriously about selling the building and the business itself."

"Selling it all?"

"Yes. I've started selling some real estate in Minnesota, and I like working with families to find homes. It feels more satisfying to me than working with businesses, and I want to continue doing it."

"How can I help with all of that?"

"You're a huge part of it, Gayle, and I know I couldn't do it without you. Just like we worked together to build it, I need you to help tear it down. I'd like you to take over running things here until we can find a buyer—and it could take a while."

"Wow, that's a *big* proposition."

They laughed.

"It is. But I'm serious, Gayle. You know how to run this business better than I do now. You know how to find good tenants, you have some help now with paperwork, and you can hire another person to do what you've been doing. I know you want to retire in a few years, but I hope we can get things settled before then. Of course, we'll increase your salary to what is appropriate."

"Wow again. It's a lot for me to think about, but I'm already getting ideas, if you want to know. Have you thought about who you might want to offer the building for sale?"

"No, I'm out of touch with who's the best these days."

"I've got some ideas, like I said; the Woodford Group comes to mind, but we'll have to do some contacting first. What's your timeline?"

Janice broke in again, "McKenzie has some extremely urgent things to deal with in Minnesota. I'm leaving the day after tomorrow and I'm hoping to take her back with me, Gayle. Do you think that could work?"

After a moment, Gayle said, "We could do that. Today and tomorrow will be full of phone calls and contacts, but we can get some balls rolling quickly enough for it to happen. We can deal with things through calls and email for quite a while. My big question is, will you both take orders from me to get it started?"

McKenzie and Janice looked at each other and smiled while both answered, "Yes!"

◆◆◆◆◆

Two hours later, Janice was at the front desk answering phones as best she could, the two clerks were computing whatever it was they computed and looking a little dazed after Gayle talked with them with a capsulized version of what had happened in the building. Janice ordered sandwiches delivered for lunch, made some great coffee, and was liking being busy. Gayle had a niece who might be qualified for the front desk position and Janice was to interview her in the afternoon before McKenzie had the final say on her hire. They were on a roll.

CHAPTER 28
CLEANING UP IN NYC

McKenzie talked with Garcia on the phone and found out there had been quite a few arrests the previous day. Word had spread about the massage parlor having "extra" services available, and surprised customers were being questioned. The police were getting some good leads on finding other trafficked girls, and Michael had broken completely, giving them more and more information. Garcia said that Michael was hoping for leniency by cooperating with the police and the Feds, but only time would tell. In truth, Michael was terrified of repercussions from some powerful people he had dealt with through the whole nasty business of trafficking.

Bernie, the doorman, was totally stressed out about everything with police all over the building for the whole previous day and evening, so McKenzie spent some time with him and Tony, the maintenance man. After their talk, both of them were happy to remain on the job until and even after she sold the building if they were needed. They respected Gayle and said they took orders from her anyway because she knew more about things than Desirée had. They were as shocked as everyone about the magnitude of trouble in which Desirée and Michael had been involved, but mistrust had been planted there, also, so it wasn't a complete surprise.

Gayle was operating out of the main corner office as ordered by McKenzie, and she said it fit her needs. The beautiful decorating had been paid for by the company anyway, as Desirée hadn't put a single personal penny into the expensive furnishings. McKenzie was fine with staying in the second office which was comfortable for her.

McKenzie already had an appointment to visit with the Woodford Group about possibly listing her building for sale, and Gayle was making calls to potential tenants for the big space in 2D plus the massage and nail salons. She already had some good leads.

When lunch arrived, the three of them met in Gayle's office and each took a deep, deep breath. Things were definitely happening and items on the To Do lists Gayle gave each of them were being checked off.

"Whew," McKenzie went, "I didn't remember what a powerhouse you really are, Gayle, can we take a minute to gobble down our ham and cheeses?"

They all laughed heartily.

"As long as you don't get mustard on my new couch," Gayle snapped. And they all laughed again.

◆◆◆◆◆

The next day went as quickly and efficiently as the one before. McKenzie had contacted two other major firms about listing her property, and she interviewed a couple of attorneys she knew from her years in New York. They were stunned to hear about Michael Romano and tried their best to assure her of their honesty. She was skittish and did check their references, people she had known before, also, and was able to decide on one to advise and represent her interests. It was a woman, Natalie Frank-Delaney, whom she had worked with on a lawsuit a few years before. Natalie won the case partly because the tenant who was sued was in the wrong, but also because Natalie was good. Gayle also knew her and approved. Another tick off the list.

Media attention was tough to deal with and reporters had been swarming the building the day before when the news broke. McKenzie did take the time to speak with them in the building's lobby. Detective Garcia was with her and had also spoken with them, and she saw the story on the late news the night before while drifting off to sleep. She stuck to repeating what he had said, and that the businesses involved were already gone and there was nothing left to see in the Ward Building. Most of them took her at her word and took pictures of the outside of the building and left. No one saw any more reporters, but they didn't know for sure that all of them were gone. Tony helped with that and did a good search in the nooks and crannies of the building.

Janice was calling all tenants from the front desk to briefly tell them what had transpired and assure them there was no danger to businesses or residents. A difficult task, but one that Janice was able to handle. A few of them came to the office to speak with Gayle or McKenzie, and they were successfully satisfied.

They would all watch the news that night and were hoping it wouldn't be too bad.

One of the calls Janice got that day from Detective Garcia surprised her because it wasn't about something on the case. In fact, it was a personal call. He said now that she was no longer involved in the murder mystery anymore, he would really like to take her to lunch so they could get to know each other better. He also asked her if she felt the same way. She was disappointed to say no to him for lunch because she had also felt the attraction. However, she told him she and McKenzie would be leaving the next day, and there was no time for lunch or anything else.

Janice was wistful when she hung up the phone. She knew he agreed, and it was a bummer on both parts that they couldn't have a date. Never say never, her mother always told her, so who knew what the future might bring.

Janice had gotten McKenzie a seat on the same afternoon flight that she was on for the following day, and packing would be a quick process that night. By six o'clock that evening, all of them were weary, but happy with their progress.

The three dynamos gathered again in Gayle's new office for celebratory wine.

McKenzie proposed a toast, "To New Adventures!" They clinked glasses and drank eagerly. After reviewing the day's crazy activities, they went down for dinner to Patisserie Alain because they didn't want to take cabs anywhere. They had a wonderful dinner and all were reassured that

Gayle was competent and willing to take over for Desirée. Not just that, but McKenzie knew her interests would be honored. Gayle's niece was determined to be suitably qualified and would be starting the next day. Detective Garcia's men had found the second set of books for Missy's Massage, and Gayle was eager to soon start reconciling things.

McKenzie was keeping her apartment until the building was sold, and she ordered it cleaned after she and Janice cleared out. What a day! And what a remarkable undertaking. They made several more toasts, clinked glasses endlessly, and smiled until they could hardly move their faces.

Exhaustion set in and they parted for the night. The next day would bring farewells and final arrangements, which they didn't yet want to think about it.

They shared a three-person group hug and went off to bed.

♦♦♦♦♦

The next morning involved final packing and preparations for traveling back to Minnesota, plus many more phone calls. McKenzie was thrilled to call Otis Jorgensen to tell him she was going home. He answered on the first ring. "Kenzie, I've been waiting for your call. Please tell me you're coming home!"

"I am. We've cleared things up here enough so I'm not needed anymore, but I have to say it was a good thing I was here. It was a terrible mess and I learned that people I thought I could trust are not who I thought they were."

"I'm sorry to hear that, Kenzie, and I hope to hear more about what you've been up against while you've been gone. Ethan really needs you, and I can't say that enough. He's still in the county jail where he's not doing well at all. I've been questioning people left and right and not getting enough information to help. The sheriff hasn't been much help, and I think he still believes that Ethan did it. That's scary. Can I pick you up at the airport?"

"You sure can if you would. Janice is with me, and I'll text you what time to pick us up. Would you also make arrangements for me to see Ethan tomorrow morning? The earlier the better. I don't just want to see him, I *need* to see him!"

"Will do. You'll be a breath of fresh air for him."

They said goodbyes and hung up, McKenzie now on the verge of tears.

◆◆◆◆◆

The day flew by and departure time came too quickly. Janice had ordered a car to the airport and goodbyes were short and painful all around. Not everything got done and the lists weren't totally checked off, but phone calls and video calls would suffice for some of their needs. McKenzie was confident in her decisions, major though they were. She knew she'd have to make some trips back to New York, but this goodbye truly felt final to her, and it was in a good way. Her future would happen in a whole new way, and she eagerly looked forward to it.

CHAPTER 29

BACK TO DEEP LAKE

McKenzie and Janice had a trouble-free flight and as they rolled their carry-ons out to the sidewalk, Otis flashed his lights after just arriving.

"Perfect timing, as always ladies," he quipped.

The girls both rolled their eyes and Janice said, "At least we don't have to tip him." They all laughed which broke what could have been a tense moment.

"I know you're eager to get home, but Mary Jo has been cooking all day and you're in for a terrific Minnesota chicken hotdish of some kind with fresh spring asparagus from our garden and a rhubarb dessert. Sound good?"

Both of them exclaimed that it sounded better than any meal they had had in New York and stopping at the Jorgensen's was a great idea.

"I can't wait to feel my arms around Goldie," McKenzie said. "Has she been good?"

"Between her and Honey, they keep our boys running all the time and just the two of them have a ball together in the back yard. They're going to miss each other when you take Goldie home."

"I'll bring her over to visit, never fear. Thank you for keeping her for me."

"Mary Jo does the work, but I know she enjoys both of the dogs, too."

Soon they made the turnoff from 694 to Deep Lake Road and headed toward the Jorgensen house. Once there, Albert and Ben, Otis's sons, and both big dogs, met them in the driveway. Total chaos ensued with barking, tail wagging, and a few jumps and whines when Goldie realized who was in the car. McKenzie dropped to her knees and hugged her dog and a few happy tears were shed and licked away.

The whole entourage surged through the back door where Mary Jo was taking a delicious looking hotdish out of the oven and heavenly smells filled the house along with loud revelry. The boys had set the dining room table and were told to light the candles so everyone could sit. Finally, everyone was seated with the dogs lying between the kitchen and dining room and carefully watching everything. Wine was poured and grace was given with grateful heads bowed.

McKenzie remembered something her mother had said years before, that saying grace was good for more reasons than being thankful for the food. It also helped the diners relax for a few moments, and leave the cares of the day behind before eating.

Immediately following the Amen the boys began digging in and passing the family-style dishes around the table. Everything was mouth-wateringly wonderful and fully enjoyed. When dessert arrived Albert and Ben gobbled theirs down and rushed off to play with the dogs before Goldie had to leave. The adults took deep breaths and rested a moment. Mary Jo had outdone herself and they all knew it. She accepted their compliments graciously and said, "I thought you might have been missing Minnesota cooking." They all agreed and Otis said, "I hope I never have to," and they laughed.

McKenzie said, "You can't imagine how glad I am to be back where I belong. I think I finally realized during this trip that Deep Lake is where my heart is and this is my forever home. I can't go into everything that happened in New York, but overall, it was an unforgettable experience with people who disappointed me more than anyone can guess. Thank you for being my true friends," she looked at Otis, Mary Jo, and Janice, "and for loving me as I do you."

They all raised their glasses with misty eyes.

McKenzie continued, "The trip wasn't all bad, I have to say. I reconnected with a wonderful friend who will be taking care of my business there until I can get things pulled together and possibly sold. I made some big decisions."

"Sold?" Otis asked. "I thought you had some good things going on there and someone was watching out for you."

With a sigh, she said simply, "Things weren't working out as well as I thought. I've decided that long-distance business isn't easy to do, and I am putting my building up for sale. I hope to focus more on my real estate business here in the future."

Janice then said, "I'll be glad to get back to my shop tomorrow, but I have to say it wasn't bad being both a private detective and a receptionist in New York City, even if only for a little while. It's a fabulous place with so much to see and do, which of course, I wasn't able to enjoy fully…but we got the job done, and that's what counts."

McKenzie said to Janice, "I'm sorry you didn't get to see much of the city, but you sure did help us this trip."

Janice snickered a little, "Who knows, there may be another trip before long. I didn't tell you that Detective Garcia and I had a couple of private conversations, and when the fur-flying was all over, he asked me for a date."

"Naw, he did?" McKenzie was surprised.

"He sure did and I would have accepted if the situation was different." Raising her brows, she added, "He's a good-looking dude, for a cop," and winked at Otis.

"And the story continues," Mary Jo said with a grin.

McKenzie just shook her head. They talked a little more about what had happened in New York, when yawns began for Janice and McKenzie, and that signaled the end of the evening. Otis drove the girls and Goldie home and verified that McKenzie could see Ethan in the jail the next morning.

◆◆◆◆◆

Early in the morning McKenzie and Goldie had already completed their first good three mile run around their usual path, and both were collapsed in happy fatigue in McKenzie's kitchen. By nine, she was showered and ready to confront locked gates and bars, and Otis picked her up in his pickup.

She was glad he was going with her to see Ethan. Going alone would have been more than she could imagine. She was beyond thankful for her life-long friendship with Otis, and that he continued to support her as well as believed in Ethan's innocence. In spite of his boss's belief that Ethan was guilty, Otis was convinced that his friend and McKenzie's much-loved significant other, simply could not have done something so heinous.

They were quiet on the ride to Stillwater, except that Otis told her to do exactly as she was told by the guards and jail staff. She didn't bring a purse and only tucked a couple of tissues in her light jacket pocket.

Entering the jail was just as confining and restricting as Otis remembered from before, and he could see the process was having a similar upsetting effect on McKenzie. They finally made it to a small room with bars on the door and were shown inside.

Ethan was already there, and he looked awful. His hair was getting a little too long and it didn't look clean. He was unshaven and his eyes were sunk into the sockets. The orange jumpsuit hung on him and he looked thin and haggard.

However, when he looked up and saw McKenzie standing there, he cried out her name and joy filled his spirit. Jail rules didn't allow them to embrace, but they sat at the scratched wooden table across from each other and were able to hold hands. Otis stood at the door to give them a smidgen of privacy, and so did the guard.

Tears were flowing for both Ethan and McKenzie and words weren't needed for several minutes as their emotions surged. Finally, Otis grudgingly approached them and said, "I'm sorry to interrupt, but we don't have long."

Ethan spoke. "These few moments have been priceless, Otis. I can never thank you enough."

"I hope you can thank me more when we figure out what happened to that guy and who is behind all of this. I am going to Fond du Lac and I want to take McKenzie with me. She has a good sense of what to look for and may be able to help me find out what we need to prove your innocence. I was going to go alone, but now she's back and I think she will be helpful. Is that okay with both of you?"

McKenzie said, "I'd love to go with Otis. Remember when he said that sleuthing was in my blood? I think it is, too, Ethan. Is it okay with you?"

"I can hardly disagree, can I? You're both right. Somebody in Fond du Lac knows what happened, I have no doubt. I didn't do this and I never saw Buddy from that horrible day in the barn until the day he came into Joe's when I was having lunch."

Otis went on, "We believe you, Ethan. We just need to find who did kill him. From your thinking, who should we start with?"

Ethan thought a moment, and said, "You should start with our old hockey coach, Jim Eastman, I think is his name. We all just called him Coach Jim. He was pretty young then, so I hope he's still teaching or at least still alive." Ethan paused and then asked, "Will you see my parents? I don't think they even know about any of this trouble. I haven't called them and now I'm stuck here. I guess they should know, huh?"

Otis answered, "Yes, they should. If it's okay with you, we'll see them and bring them up to date."

McKenzie and Otis looked at each other because they had talked earlier about the news of the whole predicament, and whether it had moved from local coverage. As far as they knew, it had stayed local.

"Yeah. This is going to be really hard for them to take."

McKenzie added, "They might be able to shed some light on this Buddy guy. You never know."

"I guess you're right." Ethan hung his head again, "They are going to be so disappointed in me. How did I get into this mess? I didn't do anything wrong and now I'm accused of murder?" His tears started again.

McKenzie's tears started again also. "We're going to get you out of this, Ethan. Mark my words, it's going to go away!"

"What about Isabella, does she know? I miss her so much!"

McKenzie closed her eyes. "You know she's with Grandma Jane and she's okay. I'm going to see her soon and will be sure she has the right information. There is hope, my love, and you have to hang on to it."

Their time was up and the guard began to usher the visitors out of the room. Leaving Ethan at that moment was excruciating for McKenzie, one of the toughest things she had ever done. She dragged herself away and when she heard the heavy crash of the solid metal door, she could hardly stand because of her sobs. Otis led her down the hall behind the quickly retreating guard, and they headed for the healing sunshine outside.

Standing there by Otis's pickup, being warmed by a beautiful spring day, McKenzie could only think that Ethan was inside, enclosed in steel, with his future uncertain. She hadn't dared to say any more about his daughter Isabella and knew he must be missing her desperately. She resolved to visit Isabella at her grandmother's in Edina because she missed her too.

Otis dropped McKenzie off at home and headed to his office to work out arrangements for their trip to Fond du Lac. He was worried about how the sheriff would take his suggestion. Sheriff Walker believed that Ethan was guilty; that the physical evidence was complete enough to verify his guilt. Otis remained convinced that Ethan was innocent and after seeing him that morning, he was even more confident.

Somehow, he needed to solve this mystery, and he hoped strongly that some solutions awaited in Ethan's hometown.

CHAPTER 30
AT HOME IN DEEP LAKE

McKenzie sat in her kitchen with Goldie at her feet and started the many phone calls she needed to make now that she was back in her world.

First, she called her office to see how things were going there.

"Minnesota's Best Real Estate," answered the receptionist.

"Hi Helen, McKenzie Ward here. Wondering if I still have a job and how things are going."

"Good to hear from you, McKenzie. You most definitely still have a job if I have anything to say about it. Are you home from your trip now?"

"Yes, I'm back from New York. I'll tell you all about it later. Is Tracey in today?"

"She sure is, hold on and I'll transfer you. Welcome home, by the way!"

Tracey Freeman was a good friend at their office in Woodbury and had been handling things with McKenzie's customers while she'd been away. Besides, Tracey and her husband Oliver were new personal friends of McKenzie and Ethan, and they'd had dinner together a few times. The four of them found lots to talk about and shared some common interests. The Freemans had a golden retriever also, and in addition, they had a son and a daughter, four-year-old twins.

Tracey picked up her phone and McKenzie said simply, "Hey Tracey, I'm back."

"Whoa, is that like in 'don't pay the ransom honey, I escaped'?"

"Yeah, pretty much. You won't believe the mess I found out there. We'll catch up later and I'm eager to tell all, but it's going to have to wait a few days."

"How long? Things have gotten busy here, it's spring, you know."

McKenzie flinched. "I know. How has it been, really? I left you with quite a burden, my friend."

"Not that bad, truth told. I'm making money hand over fist with your listings and mine, too, but my kids are beginning to wonder who that woman is who drags in when they're ready for bed."

McKenzie made a face as she heard this, "This has been a lot to put on you, I'm afraid, but the end is in sight. I just need a few more days to figure out things with Ethan, and I should be back to work."

"Ethan. I've heard the awful reports but haven't followed up on any of it. Is it as bad as the news is saying?"

"Yes, and worse. He's still in the county jail, and not doing well."

"Oh McKenzie, I'm so sorry. This must be awful for you and I can't even imagine for him. He's such a good man. It's awful for Isabella, too! How is she taking it all?"

"I haven't even talked with her yet. I'm planning to see her this afternoon if things work out. I don't even know what to say to her."

"It will come naturally. You love her and she adores you. Somehow you're going to get through all of this."

"Thank you for your kind words. I'm going with Otis to Wisconsin where Ethan and the man who was killed used to live to see what we can find out. I know Ethan didn't do what they're saying he did, and I'm determined to help Otis prove his innocence."

"You do it, girl. I've got Oliver almost trained to clean up after the kids and he's a gem at doing laundry. It's a good thing I like pink underwear. Take the time you need and there will be houses to sell later."

"Thank you is a tiny way to show my appreciation, Tracey, I hope I can do it better when this is all over."

"You will. Remember I'm a bottomless pit when it comes to wine."

Laughter and hope were hovering when they ended their call.

The next call was to Jane Rostad, Isabella's grandmother. She had a sweet little house in Edina and room for Isabella to stay, which she liked to do on occasion. Sadly, this occasion had not been planned.

Jane picked up right away, and whispered, "McKenzie. Now I know what the saying 'being on pins and needles' means, while waiting to hear what's happening with Ethan. Are you home now?"

"I am. The problems in New York City have been cleaned up as well as can be expected and they don't need me there anymore. You'll hear more about it later. More important, how is Isabella and is she there?"

"Yes, she's here, that's why I'm whispering. I didn't want to build her hopes up until I knew you were back. She misses you so much. Can you come today?"

"I surely can. Late lunch with both of you?"

"We've already had lunch, but we have some great cookies that the two of us baked yesterday. Come as soon as you can."

Both of them breathed a sigh of relief as they hung up.

Before leaving for Edina, McKenzie planned to call Otis to see if he had had any luck in getting the sheriff to go along with him on the Wisconsin visit idea. Before she could press her quick dial, the phone rang with Otis's call.

"I was just going to call you."

"Great minds think alike, my mother said. Anyway, I just got off the phone with the sheriff. As I thought, he doesn't want to go to Wisconsin, but he finally said if I was 'hell-bent' on going, that maybe I could accept things better if I went. It's a quiet time here and my deputy should be able to handle things for a couple of days without me."

"What about me going?"

"That's good news, too. He said I might as well take you along because you've got a good nose."

"A good nose, huh, let's hope it's more than that."

"It's about 300 miles to Fond du Lac, about four-and-a-half to five hours driving, less than an hour flying, but I couldn't get him to spring for flight tickets. Can you be ready to leave tomorrow morning? I know it's quick, but time is moving."

"I can if Mary Jo and the boys will keep Goldie again."

"Yeah, they don't mind that, she's a good dog. Better call Mary Jo to make sure."

"Of course, I will—right away. I'll be ready by eight, that work?"

"Gotcha. We'll take the squad car; it might wake somebody up that needs to see it. See ya tomorrow."

◆◆◆◆◆

As soon as they were off the line, McKenzie called Mary Jo. "Hey Mary Jo, it's me already asking for more favors."

"Aha, I've been expecting to hear from you. Otis was talking about going to Wisconsin and it sounds like he convinced you to go along, right?"

"You got it. Can I bring Goldie over again?"

"Of course, any time."

"I'm going to Grandma Jane's to see Isabella this afternoon and I'd love to take Goldie along. Jane's got a fenced-in yard, and I know Isabella would love to see her. How about if I drop Goldie off at your house when I get back from Jane's? That way I can at least do some laundry tonight and get ready to leave early tomorrow."

"That's perfect. The boys were going to bring back Goldie's dishes and things when they get home from school, but we'll just put that off for a few days."

"Thank you, Mary Jo, you're the best. I'm building up a lotta paybacks for some time down the road."

Mary Jo laughed, "That day might come, you never know. See you later and say 'hi' to Isabella for us. We all miss her."

"Will do," and they ended the call.

McKenzie backed her car out of the big carriage house garage. It seemed like ages since she'd driven it when it was really only a little more than a couple of weeks. Goldie was whining and turning circles in the yard, and when McKenzie opened the back door and motioned her in, she leapt in with joy.

McKenzie kept a blanket over the seat of her car to catch hair and dirt, but Goldie was a good traveler and behaved well because she knew that a car ride meant something fun was coming.

They arrived in Edina and pulled into Jane's driveway. The back door slammed open and Isabella flew to the car. She didn't know whether to hug McKenzie or Goldie first, but it turned into a group hug with lots of licking and wagging and arm flinging.

"Oh Kenzie, it's so good to see you, and thank you for bringing Goldie!" Isabella laughed.

Jane stood nearby, smiling. She didn't allow dogs in her house, but she had a great fenced-in yard, and they all went there first. Isabella and Goldie jumped around and chased each other and hugged some more. Finally, the humans settled in a beautiful yard swing, and Goldie lay at their feet with loving eyes on her young friend.

Jane started, "Is there any good news to share?"

"I got permission to see Ethan this morning. He misses you desperately, Isabella, but I'm afraid he can't see you for a while."

"I know, Grandma Jane told me. I miss him so much Kenzie. When can we go home?"

McKenzie was almost in tears herself, but she was able to stay calm and said, "It's taking longer than any of us hoped and I can't tell you when that will happen. I can tell you though, that Otis and I are leaving tomorrow for the town where your daddy used to live in Wisconsin. We'll be there a couple of days and will be looking for anything to prove his innocence."

"I know you'll do that, Kenzie. Thank you. I know my dad thanks you too."

Jane nodded, "That goes for me, too. We're fine with Isabella staying with me a while longer. We may go pick up some of her schoolwork from the school so she doesn't get too far behind. It's been a while since I was in first grade. I hope I can remember how to do the work!"

"Oh Grandma, you're so funny," Isabella laughed.

Hearing her laugh brought smiles all around in spite of the tightening band that was strangling their hearts.

They went in for cookies and milk while Goldie rested in the yard. They played a few games of checkers, a favorite of McKenzie and Isabella, and snuggled together in a chair while McKenzie read to her.

Jane fixed some soup and nummy biscuits for supper, and it came time for McKenzie to leave. They all decided that a Minnesota goodbye; one that lasts for up to half-an-hour or more, wasn't needed at that moment, so they gave quick deep hugs and kisses and before they realized it, McKenzie and Goldie were driving off.

♦♦♦♦♦

Leaving Goldie again with the Jorgensens wasn't easy, but nothing seemed to be in those days. More kisses and hugs and good wishes and McKenzie went home to prepare for the trip to Wisconsin. Would they find anything there? Was there anything to find? Time would tell, and after her chores, she fell into a troubled sleep asking God to help.

CHAPTER 31
ISSUES IN FOND DU LAC

At eight o'clock the next morning, Otis pulled into McKenzie's driveway in his squad car. At least the lights weren't flashing. She hadn't talked with any of her neighbors since leaving for New York and the whole disaster with Ethan began. She knew there were more curtains than usual moved by curious hands as they watched her comings and goings. Another thing to deal with—later.

Otis already had the Fond du Lac police department's address in his GPS, and after getting two large cups of coffee from a gas station near 694, they turned south and left Deep Lake for Highway 94.

They were silent for a long time on the road, but after an hour or so began making small talk about shared memories from when they were young. Otis brought up the time they were stealing watermelons out of a local farmer's patch, and he shot at them with a BB gun.

McKenzie reminded him, "Not one of our better ideas. At least we didn't get hit." She continued, "How about the time we tried to see how far we could skate backward on the creek that feeds the lake."

"Oboy, that was cold. I beat 'cha, but I was the first to fall in the open spot."

"I wasn't far behind. When I got home my mother had to put me in the shower to melt the ice before she could get my clothes off. Yeah, it was cold all right."

"My mom wasn't home and I had to crack the ice by myself; thought I'd never get those frozen clothes off."

"The walk home was pretty awful. Imagine how we looked! Good thing nobody saw us."

They both stiffened their arms and pretended to waddle in their seats, remembering the frozen walk and laughed till tears came.

McKenzie said, "It amazes me when I think about the stupid stuff we did as kids."

"Yeah, but we always had fun. Ya know, there's something I never told you. When we were about to start high school, I decided I should be sweet on you. The other guys were talking about girls and I didn't know any except for you, so I was starting to get up enough courage to ask you for a date."

"A date? With me?"

"Yeah, but my gramps stopped that. I don't know how he knew, but one day he said he wanted to talk. He told me he knew that I'd be thinking about girls before long and he hoped I wasn't thinking about you. He said because we'd been friends our whole lives that it just wouldn't work if we started to date. I can feel now how red my face must have been, but he went on to say that true friendships were special and that if we just stayed friends, we'd be friends forever, but if we had a date and it didn't work out romantically, it might ruin our friendship. I thought about it and decided he was right, so I never asked you."

"So that's what happened. There was a period when we didn't do so much together in early high school, and things were a little strange between us. I started dating that Andrew guy on the football team then, and I wasn't sure about you."

"I dated Leah Verhagen for a while, but she didn't understand my friendship with you, and I decided I wasn't ready for girls yet. I didn't really date until college."

"Yeah, then my mother died and I ran away to college. I'm sorry we lost all those years when I was in New York."

"Hey, life is what it is. You're back now and still my friend and I'm glad you've clicked so well with Mary Jo. I don't know what I'd do without that woman."

"Yeah, you're right, you got the right one."

"Thank God I never asked you for a date!" And they laughed some more.

They made only one comfort and gas stop, and almost five hours had whizzed by when they drove into the city of Fond du Lac, Wisconsin.

♦♦♦♦♦

Otis had done a little Internet searching to check out the city before they left on their trip. He found out the Fond du Lac Police Department was one of the larger police departments in Wisconsin and had seventy-four police officers for their population of maybe 54,000 full-time and up to 66,000 daytime population including college students and visitors who left town at night. Quite a difference compared to Deep Lake's basic rent-a-cop which included himself and one deputy on loan from the Washington County Sheriff's Department. He was impressed, to say the least.

They were a little early to meet the chief for their one-thirty appointment, so they drove around the city to get a feel for the land, as Otis put it. They drove through beautiful Lake Winnebago's Lakeside Park and saw the Octagon Lighthouse that was a focal point of the park. Out of commission after many years of marking the entrance to the harbor entrance, it had been restored beautifully by the City.

The lake itself, Otis learned, was the largest lake in the U.S. entirely within the state, about thirty miles long and ten miles wide. However, the lake was shallow with a maximum depth of only twenty-one feet, compared to their small town's Deep Lake which had a huge hole at one end as deep as 140 to 150 feet. The result of a retreating glacier, there must have been a really big chunk of ice down there at one time.

They got out of the squad car and walked a little to stretch out. It was obviously a well-cared for city. Otis wondered where Ethan's father's bait shop was and if it was close to the lake. They would call his parents after they had spoken with the police chief, or maybe later after they checked into their motel.

♦♦♦♦♦

Otis and McKenzie met with Police Chief Samuel Webster. He was a big man, in all directions. He had a full head of brown hair, dark eyes, and pockmarked skin. Even his voice was big, and loud. He was dressed in full police uniform, including a wide belt with several pieces of equipment attached, and a black leather holster holding a lethal-looking weapon. At their introduction, Otis told him how impressed he was with the city from what he'd seen so far. Even the police headquarters were in a fairly new and well-kept brick building. It was apparent the support they gave the city was well-returned.

"That's good to hear, we try hard. So, you're an assistant sheriff for Washington County in Minnesota, right?" Near the Twin Cities?"

"That's right. Please call me Otis like everyone does."

"Well, I'm just plain Sam around here."

"Thank you, Sam. This is McKenzie Ward, a Realtor from Minnesota. She's a close friend of the man from here that we're investigating, Ethan Thompson."

Sam and McKenzie nodded at each other.

Sam spoke up, "From our phone call, I understand this Thompson went to school here and graduated in 1997. You say a bunch of boys from the hockey team got in some trouble around graduation time and you want to know more about that issue."

"That's right," Otis agreed. "We're hoping you can steer us to someone who might be able to shed some light on what really happened and maybe who the boys were that were involved."

"Yeah, that's what you said. I wasn't here myself at that time; came in '02, but I think I know who might be able to help you."

Both Otis and McKenzie brightened.

"The local high school is new now, the Fond du Lac High School was founded in 2001. Before that the old school was called Goodrich High School, and that's where this Thompson kid graduated. The school was old, but it was kept up and they had a good hockey team from what I've heard."

Otis said, "Thompson said the coach was just called Coach Jim, but he thinks his name might have been Eastman."

"Got 'cha one better on that—his name was Herstman, Jim Herstman, according to the school records. One of my guys on the force was on the hockey team with Thompson and he remembers them."

McKenzie broke in, "That's terrific, Sam, can you tell us how we can get in touch with this man?"

"Sure can. He's a member of our K-9 Unit, works with his dog and I swear that sucker can smell drugs a mile away. We got two K-9 Units now and they're worth every penny we spent on 'em."

Otis repeated, "And how can we reach him?"

"Oh yeah, I told him you were coming, and he's gonna be here at the station about four, he said."

"Four o'clock here, today? That's great!" Otis exclaimed.

Sam said, "I thought you'd be happy about that."

McKenzie added, "We have to make a call or two now, and we could come back at four if that would work for you."

Sam agreed, "That's okay with me. The guy's name is Doug Weyerhauser, dog is Buster. I'll be gone by that time, but just ask at the desk and they'll get Doug for you."

"That's great," Otis said again. He was so glad there was someone to talk with who could possibly verify Ethan's story. "Oh, also, Sam, before we go, we're going to talk with Ethan Thompson's parents, Joyce and Luke Thompson. I understand they own a bait shop somewhere near the lake."

"Yeah, 'Luke's' they call it. It's one of the better bait shops around, and I get bait there myself from time to time. Used to be a teacher, Luke did, and bought the bait shop when he retired."

"Yes, that's them," McKenzie said. "We have their phone number."

"Well, that's about what I know for now," Sam said. "I have to make a trip up the lake, so if you wanna stop by again tomorrow for any help, just let me know."

Otis shook Sam's hand and said, "You've already been a big help. We appreciate everything you've done, and at least we've got somewhere to start."

◆◆◆◆◆

Outside in the parking lot, Otis and McKenzie were thrilled with what they had learned from Sam. "What a down-to-earth guy he is," Otis began. "He sure knows his town."

"That he does. However, what we didn't ask him and should have, is how does he know Buddy Kraus."

"You're right. I clean forgot to ask him because I was too excited about the K-9 guy. I bet he does know him."

"I think so, too. And I wonder how he knows him." McKenzie pondered.

CHAPTER 32
QUESTIONS IN FOND DU LAC

Otis and McKenzie decided to drive the short distance back to Lakeside Park and relax there for a short time before meeting with Doug Weyerhauser at the police station. While there, they phoned Ethan's parents. A hard call to make because the parents didn't yet know about what had happened with Ethan—and had no idea he was in jail at that moment. McKenzie was the one to call, as hearing from a law officer might scare them even more.

When Mr. Thompson answered the call, McKenzie introduced herself as a close friend of Ethan and Isabella.

He said, "Oh yes, Ethan mentioned you a while back. We are looking forward to meeting you when the time comes. Don't know when we're going to get to Minnesota, it's a long trip."

"Yes, it is a drive, Mr. Thompson. Actually, I'm here in Fond du Lac right now with another friend of Ethan's, Otis Jorgensen. I think you might have met on another occasion."

"I guess we did, he's that sheriff fellow, but it was a while ago. Is Ethan not with you today? Is everything all right there?"

"That's why I'm calling, Mr. Thompson. Ethan is fine for right now, but there has been an incident, and we'd like to talk with you and Mrs. Thompson about it."

"An incident? What sort of incident? Is Isabella okay?"

"Isabella is fine, and Otis and I would like to come to your home later this afternoon to let you know what has been happening with Ethan. We have your address. Is it okay for us to come by about five-thirty or so to talk with the two of you?"

They could hear Mrs. Thompson in the background as her husband said loudly, "Joyce, come here, something's going on with Ethan! An 'incident' they said…" He came back on the phone and said, "What's that? Five-thirty you say? Yes, we'll be here. Can we talk to Ethan now?"

"Ethan isn't here right now, but he may be calling you in a few days. Otis and I will see you at your home at five-thirty. Thank you so much."

McKenzie slumped, "Well, that didn't go well. I'm sorry I messed it up so badly."

Otis replied, "There wasn't much you could do any different. We have really bad news for them that we can't sugarcoat. My GPS says they live about twenty, twenty-five minutes from the police station. I hope we can get everything done there by five."

"We have to. That's the most important thing we have to do today."

"It's all important if we're going to get Ethan out of this mess. Back to the police station for now."

◆◆◆◆◆

They walked into the police station and there to greet them were Doug Weyerhauser and his dog. "Sheriff Jorgensen?" Weyerhauser put out his hand.

Otis replied, "Well, that's Assistant Sheriff, but you can just call me Otis. This is McKenzie Ward, my uh, associate from Minnesota."

McKenzie was okay with associate and shook hands with Weyerhauser too. "I'm McKenzie."

Weyerhauser said, "Call me Doug, and this is Buster," gesturing to the handsome German Shepherd sitting at his side. "He's off duty now, so you can pat him if you like. He's pretty friendly."

McKenzie turned slightly to the side and put her hand down in a loose fist so Buster could smell her first. Ethan had taught her how to approach a strange dog, and it seemed to be working. Buster wagged his tail and moved a step closer to her after several sniffs, so she gently rubbed his neck and side, making her his forever friend.

Doug said, "Somebody taught you well, McKenzie, you know how to greet a strange dog."

"That would be Ethan Jorgensen, our vet in Deep Lake."

"I remember him well, Ethan. Nice guy but pretty quiet, and he could be a little nerdy in high school. He studied a lot."

McKenzie continued, "That sounds like him. He and I are extremely close and we need your help to get him out of a bad situation right now."

Otis interrupted and asked, "Doug, is there a place here where we could talk privately? We have a lot of questions for you, if you don't mind."

"Of course, just follow me." And he led them to a small room with a table and chairs. They all sat down and Buster laid down at Doug's feet. "Ask away. I know a little about the situation, and I understand that Buddy Kraus has been killed. Chief Sam filled me in some."

Otis started, "Sam told us that you graduated with Ethan and were on the same hockey team. That right?"

"Yup, we played hockey for several years together. It's the main game here with all the ice we have in the winters. We've had good coaching, too, through the years. Our last coach was Coach Jim Herstman. He's retired now, but still lives in town."

"Yes, we're hoping to talk with him also, to find out what we can about the dynamics of the team and how you guys worked together."

"Dynamics, huh? We played pretty well together; won a lotta games and most everybody seemed to do their part."

"You said that Ethan was a little nerdy. How did he fit in with the rest of the team?"

"I didn't mean that in a bad way. He was quiet and didn't like to party as much as some of us. He was smart and I knew he'd do well for himself. He's a vet, huh? A good one?"

"The best," Otis said, and glanced at McKenzie. "Tell us what you know about Buddy Kraus."

Doug shook his head. "Buddy never did turn out good. He was what you might call the weakest link in the chain on our hockey team. Didn't like teamwork and tried too hard to be a star. Never went to college or even trade school and for a long time had trouble keeping jobs."

"What can you tell us about the barn-burning incident toward the end of your senior year?"

"You know about that, huh?"

"We do. Ethan told us all about it."

"He did. Well then, I might not be able to tell you much more. I was there along with the other guys. Must have been about a dozen of us that day and we were celebrating the end of the school year. Don't know who suggested that place, might have been somebody's relative. Anyway, a fire got started and the barn started burning. We didn't know an old horse was in the back of the barn and it started screaming. Never heard anything so awful in my life, that screaming. We all ran outta there as fast as we could, but Ethan, crazy about animals as he was, ran back in there to try to save that horse. He was nuts to do it, but he ran back in that burning barn. Some guys ran after him and pulled him out just before the whole thing collapsed. The horse stopped screaming then, and Ethan cried in front of all of us." Doug stopped a moment and shook his head.

"We got back to town and some of us told our dads. I know I told mine. The dads went to talk with the police chief, and that's the last any of us ever heard about the fire. It was determined to be an accident and none of us ever talked about it again."

"Wow, what an awful experience for all of you to end your school years."

"Yeah, we split up then and all went our own ways after that. After college I became a cop and been one ever since. Just started this K-9 business a couple of years ago, and really like it."

"What do you know about the other guys who were at the fire? What has happened to them?"

"Well, we've had school reunions but not everybody goes to them, so I'm not sure about some of the guys. I know Buddy turned out to be an asshole—sorry about the language McKenzie—but he always was. He was married to a nice gal, Linda was her name, but she had a baby that wasn't quite right, and Buddy was mean as hell to both of them. She left him and moved away with the kid. The rest of Buddy's family was okay and they still live up the lake a ways. In fact, Chief Sam is married to Buddy's sister."

"He is?" McKenzie broke in.

"Yeah, there's a bunch of Krauses up near the western middle part of the lake. Pretty nice people except for Buddy."

McKenzie and Otis looked at each other, and Otis went on, "You've been helpful to us, Doug, but we still don't know who might have killed Buddy. Do you have any ideas?"

"Coulda been anybody. Like I said, Buddy wasn't a good guy and he coulda had a lotta enemies."

"Do you know of anyone in particular who might have had it in for Buddy? Someone he treated badly or something like that?"

"Well, there was one guy, one of our hockey teammates, Hank Overby it was. He works on cars and has his own small repair shop outside of town. He came to Chief Sam one day and said Buddy came to him and said he had pictures of Hank and the rest of us starting the fire in the barn that time. Said Buddy was trying to blackmail him to keep quiet about it. Hank came to Chief Sam who told him the statute of limitations on that had run out years ago and there was nothing Buddy could do. Never heard anything more about it. I know that Hank sure had no time for Buddy before or after that."

Again, McKenzie and Otis looked at one another. They needed to compare notes about what they learned from Doug, and it was getting on toward five o'clock. Otis ended the interview with Doug and thanked him for the information he shared. He asked him if they could talk again if needed, and he was fine with that. They all shook hands, McKenzie leaned down and patted Buster again and she and Otis headed for their car.

◆◆◆◆◆

They needed to get to the Thompson's soon, so there wasn't time for Otis and McKenzie to digest all they heard from Doug Weyerhauser; it would have to wait.

When they pulled up in front of Luke and Joyce's home, another car was in the driveway. A woman about Ethan's age came out to meet them.

"I'm Ethan's sister, Bethany. I take it you're the sheriff and Ethan's girlfriend?"

Otis answered, "We are. Make that assistant sheriff. I'm Otis Jorgensen and this is McKenzie Ward. We're here to fill you in on what's happened with Ethan."

"My parents are beside themselves and don't know what is going on. Mom keeps calling Ethan's cell phone and when he doesn't answer, she cries. My husband and I live nearby and we got a sitter so we could come over to hear what's happened. Come on in."

The elder Thompsons and Bethany's husband were seated in the living room of the mid-sized stand-alone townhome in a nice part of town. Introductions were made, and they learned Bethany's husband was Aaron Gifford, an accountant with his own small CPA firm. They all sat down and because of the tension, no one even thought about drinks or offering food or anything.

McKenzie knew from Ethan that the Giffords had three small children, and she told Bethany how glad she was to finally meet her and would love to meet her children as well.

"I'd like that, too, McKenzie. Ethan has raved about you when we talked on the phone, but that has been too long ago and now we're so worried."

Otis started the explanations. "That's why we're here, Bethany, and all of you. Ethan is in an unbelievably bad situation right now. I'm going to be blunt and tell everything so you know exactly what we're up against. It started with his vet clinic being badly vandalized. Drugs were stolen and the next night a man was found murdered with a large animal tranquilizer. The syringe had Ethan's fingerprints on it. The man was Buddy Kraus from here in Fond du Lac, who Ethan says had earlier tried to blackmail him. At this point, Ethan has been accused of murdering Kraus, and he is incarcerated in the county jail in Stillwater, Minnesota."

Joyce wailed, "My…Ethan…is in jail?"

Bethany went to her mother and put her arms around her.

McKenzie said, "That's why we came to tell you, we couldn't just use the telephone to deliver this terrible news. Ethan asked us to tell you because he couldn't do it himself."

The shock in the room was almost palpable, and profound silence lasted a full minute or more.

Finally, the dad asked, "Do you think he did it?"

"No!" Otis and McKenzie said in unison. Otis went on. "We know that Ethan is not capable of doing this terrible crime. We believe that someone else has made things look like Ethan did this, and we're determined to find out who."

Bethany asked, "Where is Isabella in all this?"

McKenzie said, with tears starting, "She's with her Grandma Jane in Edina, less than a half-hour away from Deep Lake, and she's fine. I saw her yesterday and we had a lovely time together. You should know that I love Isabella like she was my own."

"Thank you," her grandmother said. "I miss her so much."

The atmosphere was turning maudlin, so Otis asked, "Do you know of anyone who might bear a grudge against your son? Someone who may be looking for a way to punish him or have some deep-seated resentment for him? We're looking at every possibility we can to prove his innocence."

Luke said, "It's so hard to think about things like that, and Ethan has been away from here for a long time. He and Elizabeth moved to Minnesota after they married and he started his veterinary practice there. My own parents had moved there for my father's job some years ago. Dad passed away and my mother decided to stay because she loved the community. She invited Ethan and Elizabeth to live with her until they got settled in the town, and he built his vet clinic. When she passed away from old age they stayed in her house. You most likely know the rest, that Elizabeth died and Ethan has raised Isabella on his own."

Otis said, "I've known Ethan since he came to Deep Lake, and we've become close friends. He's a good man and I just can't imagine anyone wanting to harm him. We have to be realistic and understand that someone has done just that—framed him for the death of Buddy Kraus."

Aaron spoke up. "There are quite a few members of the Kraus family around this area. I remember that Buddy was not a successful man and he stiffed me when I did some tax work for him some years ago. Never paid his bill and we finally had to write it off."

McKenzie added, "That's what we're learning. We also just found out that the local police chief is married to Buddy's sister."

Otis said, "We'll be checking that out tomorrow. We may visit some of his relatives, awkward as it might be. The family brought Buddy back here for the funeral last week. Tell me, what do you remember about the barn-burning incident that happened around the time of Ethan's high school graduation?"

Joyce and Luke looked at each other and frowned. Luke said, "It was a terrible thing. He told me as soon as he got home, and I was one of the fathers who went to the police about it. I think it was rightly handled and determined to be an awful accident. The farmer never pressed charges, but Ethan was crushed by the death of that old horse. He never really got over it, poor kid."

"Do you remember who the other boys were who were involved in the incident?"

"No, not really."

Joyce spoke up, "I have Ethan's old high school yearbook. Maybe we could look at the pictures and remember some of the boys."

She got the yearbook and they all looked at the pictures of the graduates and found the hockey team was also pictured. From that photo they were able to identify most of the boys who might have been at the party with Ethan and Buddy. Luke had a copy feature on his printer, so they printed some copies of the team picture.

It was getting late and McKenzie and Otis needed to check in at their hotel, so they brought the visit to an end. It had been a hard, but good time together, and the two of them wanted to gather their thoughts, as well as get something to eat. Leaving Ethan's family was an emotional time, so they did it as quickly as possible.

At the end, Bethany said, "None of us has had time or thoughts collected enough to think about dinner. How about coming back here for dinner tomorrow evening after your day of searching for possibilities? We'll all do some thinking, too, and may come up with something."

"Great idea," Otis answered. "We hope to be in town maybe two nights so that works out for us."

♦♦♦♦♦

In the car after leaving, McKenzie said, "What a lovely family. I knew Ethan came from good stock."

Otis agreed, "You're right. They're in pain right now but I sure hope they can help us. This is getting more and more interesting, and I'm eager to dig more into the whole Kraus family dynamics. Don't know about you, but I'm pooped. It's been a long day. Eat something light at the hotel and then crash?"

McKenzie agreed and they got checked into adjoining rooms and met later in the hotel's dining room. They were almost too tired to eat but did have sandwiches. Their individual minds were whirling with what they had learned and decided to talk when they met for breakfast the next morning.

♦♦♦♦♦

Early the next day found McKenzie and Otis eating at the hotel's buffet that featured waffles and omelets to order, so both were happy. They shared what each had learned from the previous day's episodes.

With his mouth full of blueberry waffle and whipped cream, Otis mumbled, "The Kraus family is my priority."

"Mine, too," McKenzie said while sipping a delicious latte and digesting her vegetable omelet. "Do we call Chief Sam first? He has some questions to answer about why he didn't tell us about his connection to the Krauses."

"Yeah, he's first on the list, and his reactions might determine where we go next. I'll call him before we leave here after breakfast. By the way, I booked us for one more night here. I sure hope we find something today because this time tomorrow we may be on our way back home."

"I hope so. I need some home-time after my New York trip."

They finished up their breakfast and Otis said, "Meet you in the lobby in thirty minutes?"

"Gotcha."

♦♦♦♦♦

McKenzie was in the lobby in thirty minutes, with no sign of Otis. She walked outside and saw the squad car where they had parked it. As she walked toward it, the car looked odd, like one side was higher than the other. When she got closer she saw that Otis had used the jack to raise one side of the car and was changing a tire.

"What's going on here—got a flat tire?"

"Two of them," he grunted.

"Two! How could we have two flat tires?"

"That's my question. Somebody doesn't want us here is the obvious answer."

"That's not good."

"No, it isn't. Somebody from here is worried about us finding out something, or someone might have followed us here from home. Our squad car isn't exactly anonymous."

"You're right about that." McKenzie nervously looked around.

"They're long gone now. This was done during the night, and it looks like they just let the air out, the tires aren't damaged near as I can tell. I keep this handy air pressure thing in the trunk and with a USB connection I can fill the tires.

Otis said he had already contacted Chief Sam. Sam had opened the conversation saying he knew they would find out about his connection to the Kraus family and he wanted to explain. He invited the two of them back to his office at the main police station as soon as they could get there.

"Well, that's a good thing, right?"

Otis replied, "I sure hope so. Things seem to be getting deeper all the time."

They headed right to the station nearby.

Sam, looking bigger than ever, welcomed them in the lobby and led them to his office straight away. After the good-mornings, he started. "I know you're upset with me that I didn't tell you yesterday about being related to the Kraus family. I think you just forgot to ask me about how I knew Buddy, but I let it go, knowing I'd be talking with you about it today.

"The Kraus family occupies a big area up the lake off Highway 45. In fact, there's so many Krauses around they call it Krausville, although it isn't officially named that. It's a small unincorporated village with a church and a few stores, a bar and a couple of restaurants. Others live there, too, of course, but there's a lotta Krauses. Big family.

"Anyway, yes, I'm married to Buddy Kraus's sister, Emily. We went to school together and she's a good woman. We've got four kids and it's a good family. Em's brother Buddy was a misfit from the beginning. The guy was just born bad; in trouble from when he was just a little guy from what I learned through the years. He was the youngest and got everything he wanted—and he wanted everything."

Sam stopped and shook his head with a frown. "He's done that sort of thing before where he tries to get people to give him money. He'd figure out some way to blackmail people with pictures or stories or something. This time it seemed to get him killed. All of us thought that Ethan Thompson really did kill him, so we were all okay with him being jailed for it. You guys released the body and we had Buddy's funeral last week. Feelings about Thompson aren't too good in Krausville right now."

Otis and McKenzie were nodding.

"When you two showed up yesterday after our phone call and told me how seriously you believed Thompson to be innocent, I began to wonder. Last night I had a sort of come-to-Jesus meeting with as many Krauses as I could get hold of. Of course, every one of them insisted Thompson did it, but I'm wondering about some of them. You know that Kraus's wife left him, right?"

"Yes, Doug Weyerhauser told us that."

"Do you know where she is?"

"No, we don't," Otis admitted.

"She's in Deep Lake, Minnesota. Her name is Linda Peterson, her maiden name, and she has a son named Timmy." I made it a point to know where she went, just in case, I guess."

Otis thought a moment and said, "That's Linda from the bank. Timmy has Down syndrome and works at Joe's restaurant. Yes, we know them, or know of them at least. I talked with Timmy after Ethan's lunch with Buddy. Timmy certainly didn't seem to know that Buddy was his father."

"Doesn't surprise me," Sam went on. "Buddy was vicious with both of them."

"So she was Buddy's wife? I wonder why she came to Deep Lake?" McKenzie asked.

"That's one thing we have to find out," Otis said, "when we get back there. Do you have any more surprises for us, Sam?"

"I don't. At this point, I don't know who did Buddy in. You two seem so confident that Ethan didn't do it, it shakes me up. I'm an honest cop," looking Otis in the eye, "and I'm tough on crime. If it was somebody from here or someone from the Kraus family, I'll find out, I swear to you."

"I want to believe you, Chief Sam," Otis said. "I think you've been honest with us. We'll leave one of these photos with you of the boys that could have been involved in the country party when the barn got burned. Please share it with Doug and anyone else you can think of to see if you can find another clue. Ethan Thompson did not kill Buddy Kraus, and I can guarantee that with my own job. My boss thinks he did it, but McKenzie and I know he didn't."

McKenzie spoke up, "We plan to leave here tomorrow morning unless we find something more worth looking at. You have our number, so please call if you find out anything at all."

"You know I will. Linda also has a big family, and there's a bunch of Petersons around Krausville, too. I'll check them out to see if any of them know anything."

"Is it worth us going there today and talking with any of them?" Otis asked. "We were thinking of doing that."

"You're strangers and too close to the man most of them believe killed Buddy. Even though Buddy wasn't well liked in the community, family loyalty means a *lot* in this area."

Otis agreed. "I think you're right. If you're truly on our side, and I badly want to believe that, I trust you to find justice." Looking around, Otis added, "You run a tight ship here, Sam, and I think you're a good cop. I hope you're as good as we think you are."

Standing and offering his hand, Sam said, "I hope so, Otis and McKenzie, you too. Let's find this bugger and put this whole thing to rest."

"Thank you, Chief Sam. I think we'll look for another one or two of the guys who were at the fire and talk with them this afternoon if we can and leave for Deep Lake in the morning. Work for you?"

"Yeah, and if you show that photo to my deputy at the desk or we'll call Doug in again, they may be able to steer you where you want to go. Must be several of them still in town."

"Thanks again, that's what we'll do. We're having dinner with Mr. and Mrs. Thompson tonight and we'll talk more with them."

"Luke was a shop teacher for the junior high for a long time and should know most of those guys. Maybe he can shed some light on things."

"Good thought. We'll talk later." And McKenzie and Otis left Sam's office.

They went to the front desk and got more copies of the photo of the hockey team. The uniformed officer there didn't recognize any of the boys, but he did call Doug to stop in around noon, and they would talk more with him."

Walking to their car, McKenzie asked, "Do you believe him?"

"I really want to. He's tougher than an old boot and I wouldn't want him glaring at me with questions. I hope he can put the fear of God in the Krauses."

"I do, too. Otis, let's get some coffee before we meet with Doug. We may not get any lunch today."

◆◆◆◆◆

At noon, they were back at the police station and Doug Weyerhauser and Buster met them in the lobby. Buster recognized them and wagged his tail at McKenzie who immediately gave him a good pat on his side. He leaned into her and smiled as only dogs can smile.

It turned out that Doug not only knew some other guys from the original hockey team, but he called one of them who was a friend and lived in town, and he came to the station. Doug had prepped him a little on the case so he knew about the murder of Buddy and that Ethan was being charged with it. Charles O'Brien was a plumber with his own shop. After

Trouble in Deep Lake ◆ 179

introductions, he told them to call him Chuck, and he wouldn't charge them plumber rates for his interview; he was on his lunch break.

They all laughed and McKenzie said she wouldn't try to sell him a house, either.

They sat at the conference table where they had talked the day before, with photos of the hockey team spread before them.

Otis started the conversation, "Doug and Chuck, this murder of Buddy Kraus seems to be getting deeper and deeper. We're hoping that you can help with any small piece of information you can think of. We believe Ethan Thompson is not guilty of this crime and we're looking for proof."

Chuck agreed, "From what I remember about Thompson is that he couldn't be guilty. He's a great guy and would give anyone the shirt off his back; he couldn't murder anybody. The way he cried at the death of that old horse in the barn was enough to stick with anyone. I think that's why he became a vet, from what I remember."

McKenzie said, "That's what we think, too, but what we need is positive proof that he didn't do it. Someone has gone to great lengths to pin the crime on him—we believe he's being framed for this murder."

"Wow, that's serious, huh?" Chuck replied.

Otis took over, "Yes, it is serious. What can you tell us about your interactions with Buddy Kraus and others on your hockey team? Is there anyone in the group who you think might be capable of murder for the right reasons?"

Doug added, "Most of these guys have moved away for their jobs or other reasons, and just aren't around to ask. The only really bad guy was Buddy. As you know already, he was a total jerk when it came to getting his way. He was so tough about getting what he wanted that nobody wanted to cross him."

Chuck said, "I heard that he was into gambling a while back."

"Gambling? On what?" Otis asked.

"Cars. He loved fast cars. One time he asked me and another guy to go with him to Road America over near Elkhart Lake. We had a hell of a day watching one of the NASCAR Xfinity races. I know Buddy knew a bookmaker who took bets on the races and I know he placed some bets. I saw him do it, but I didn't have the guts or the money. I sort of shut my eyes to what he was doing. I couldn't take time off to do that again, but that one time was great."

"That's good to know, Chuck. Thanks for telling us. Anything else like that sort of thing?" Otis asked.

Doug added, "I didn't know that about the gambling on fast cars, but it doesn't surprise me. Buddy used to bet on little things, like how many hockey games we would win or lose and I saw him collecting money from some of the guys that got suckered in. That guy was really bent."

"Yeah, he was." Chuck said, "I hate to talk bad about the dead, but he was up for anything that would give him money and hurt somebody else. That's just how it was."

The four of them talked further about Buddy's wife and son, but Chuck and Doug had pretty much severed contact with Buddy by then. They did know Linda Peterson and her family and felt sorry that she had married Buddy. They knew it would not be good for her. Neither of them seemed to know why Linda had gone to Minnesota or even that she had after she left Buddy.

They ended the session after an hour and a half or so, and Chuck went back to work. Doug and Buster had a job to search for an elderly man who had walked away from a care facility. Apparently, that was a good share of the work he and his dog did, and McKenzie found it so sad because often they found the person when it was too late.

♦♦♦♦♦

Otis wanted to touch base with Coach Jim Herstman, and they had a couple of hours before going to the Thompsons. He called the retired coach and was lucky to get him at home. Coach invited them to come for a short interview.

Coach Jim lived with his wife in another townhome development for fifty-five-plus folks and was enjoying retirement. With introductions at the door, they were invited to be seated in the living room. Mrs. Herstman left to make tea for all of them, and they started the discussion.

Otis began, "We're investigating the murder of Buddy Kraus which happened in Minnesota. Ethan Thompson is being held in the Washington County Jail for the crime, but McKenzie and I don't think Ethan did this, and we're looking for any help we can find to see who might have done it."

"Wow," Coach Jim said. "This goes back a while, but I sure do remember that class. If anyone would get himself murdered from that exceptional class, I have to say it would be Buddy Kraus. No matter how much we stressed teamwork and working together and making the other guy look good, Buddy lived life for one person, himself.

"On their hockey team, he was constantly looking for ways to make himself a star. They were a good team overall, but would have been a hell of a lot better if Buddy could have suppressed his own personal ambitions. But he couldn't, and they turned out to be an average team. That's just the way it goes. For Ethan Thompson to be accused of killing Buddy, I find that really hard to believe. Ethan was the definition of a teammate and he worked as hard as Buddy, but at making the team succeed and all his team members look good instead of himself. He was just the all-around good guy. How could this have happened?"

Otis and McKenzie filled him in on what had transpired, along with their suspicions that Ethan had been set up or framed for the murder.

"Framed? By who? Buddy was a jerk, I have to say, but murder? It looks like somebody really wanted him dead."

"We've heard that Buddy liked to gamble. Can you confirm that?" Otis asked.

"Buddy didn't like to gamble, he loved it. He would take bets on who could throw their towels and hit the basket. He bet on whose dirty socks smelled the worst. Anything."

"Did you have any contact with Buddy after that school year?"

"Not really, except that he came to see me once about sponsoring him in some sort of truck rally or something. He drove the big rigs for a while, but it didn't last like everything didn't last with Buddy. I told him I had to think about it and by the time I decided to take a chance on him, he had already withdrawn from the competition."

"Did you know his wife or child?"

"I didn't know he was married, sorry."

Mrs. Herstman brought a tray of tea with some tiny shortbread cookies, and they all helped themselves.

Otis asked Coach Jim, "Is there anything else that you knew or found out about Buddy that might help us to find his killer?"

"I'm afraid not, except, wait a minute. One of the boys on our hockey team came from a farm family. He's taken over the farm now and is successful at it. Nice fella. He called me one day and said that Buddy was trying to get money from him about that barn-burning incident the boys got into near graduation time. I told him to ask the police chief about it because there were no charges in the incident and there shouldn't have been any way Buddy could extort money because of it. Make sense to you?"

"It does because we know of at least one more incident like that. Buddy was devious and tried to get money out of people any way he could."

"If I think of anyone else who might help you or anything I missed, I'll call you. It's a real shame about Ethan. Can't imagine him doing anything like a murder, for God's sake. What a mess for him."

"You're right," Otis concluded, "Here's a card with the number to call if you think of anything. Thanks for your time. By the way, the team members we've talked with say you were a good coach."

Herstman gave a grimacing smile as they left.

Otis and McKenzie went back to the hotel to rest and think a while before they went to the Thompsons for an early dinner.

◆◆◆◆◆

Arriving at the Thompson home, they were assailed by three young sets of arms, legs, and voices the moment they came in the door. Bethany and Aaron had brought their children to see their grandparents. They also might have thought it would lighten the atmosphere with McKenzie and Otis there to counteract the heaviness in the house because of what had happened with their Uncle Ethan.

Talk was mainly about family and activities and hoped-for future gatherings, and questions about when they'd see their cousin, Isabella.

When asked if they had made progress that day, Otis said, "We have learned some new lines of inquiry, and that is a big help. We spoke with the coach and another member of the hockey team, Chuck O'Brien, and we learned Buddy liked to gamble."

Luke bypassed the gambling comment but said, "Good man, O'Brien, he's our plumber."

McKenzie and Otis left after Joyce's wonderful dinner, saying they would be in contact when they got back to Deep Lake, and they'd try to work out a phone call for them with Ethan.

CHAPTER 33
RETURN TO DEEP LAKE

On their ride back to Deep Lake, Otis and McKenzie were deep in their own private thoughts, but they also talked about possible suspects and scenarios. They each offered potential possibilities, and some remote opinions as well. They included ideas about other members of the long-ago hockey team, possible gangster connections to Buddy Kraus, and even questioned the validity of Police Chief Samuel Webster, or Chief Sam as he was known. His closeness to Buddy's family could surely be in question.

McKenzie then said, "Let's talk about Linda Peterson. Do you think she could have smashed the clinic and killed Buddy?"

"I don't know much about her or if she's strong enough to have done it. I don't think Timmy helped. From my short talk with him at Joe's, he would have let something slip. I didn't catch anything unusual in what he said—except now that I really think about it, he said something about his name being different. He told me his full name was Timothy Peterson, and then said it used to be different. I was thinking that he's called Timmy instead of Timothy, but he might have meant that his last name was Kraus and now is Peterson. My bad that I didn't catch that."

"Well, now you did, so we can ask Linda about it. I wonder about Linda's knowledge of drugs. Do you think she knew enough to pick the right drug to kill Buddy? Maybe she had help crashing the clinic, and even in killing Buddy."

"Yeah, that's a good idea. We'll follow-up on that for sure. Remember she has a big family back in Krausville and maybe one of them helped her. I wanted to go there yesterday to talk with some of them, but Chief Sam discouraged it. Now I think I should have insisted, and I may have to take a second trip there as things work out."

"Not without me. I really like Ethan's family and want to see them again. I feel so bad for all of them to think about him sitting in jail. *I* feel bad for him sitting in jail." She gave a big sigh. Do you think we'll ever get this figured out?"

"We have to. Things have been skewed so well to make it look like Ethan did it, I think a trial would be hopeless."

"I'm afraid you're right. Looks like it's up to us to find out what really happened."

McKenzie hesitated and continued reluctantly, "Okay, let's be really brutal here. You and I know Ethan the best of anyone right now, but the evidence is almost overwhelming. Do you think it's even remotely possible that Ethan really did this?"

Otis gulped and sighed deeply. "Yes, we do know Ethan best, and I for one know he is simply not capable of doing what he's being accused of. No matter how angry he could be or how much someone could provoke him, he couldn't have done this. It's simply not in his genetic makeup, period."

McKenzie grinned and looked at him, "Well said, my friend. We're on the same page."

Otis replied, "Yeah, it's up to us." He scowled and focused on his driving.

◆◆◆◆◆

Back in Deep Lake after noon and under a beautiful blue sky, Otis dropped McKenzie off at her house, and headed for his office. His plan was to contact Linda Peterson right away to see what she had to say. McKenzie had phone calls to make and needed to pick up her dog, so they both had a busy day ahead. It seemed obvious they were both thinking about visiting Ethan again, but didn't talk about it, likely because it was just too painful in light of seeing his family so recently.

McKenzie called her office and asked for one more day before she dived into her work again. She then called Mary Jo and was invited for coffee and cookies and some girl talk that she knew she would really appreciate. She headed there first.

♦♦♦♦♦

When Otis got to his office, his deputy, Lloyd, said while Otis and McKenzie had been in Wisconsin, he received a strange call that was routed through the St. Paul Police Department. Apparently, someone from a Motel 6 had called them. They had seen an article in the paper and recognized the name of a murdered man. They said the man had stayed one night in the motel and had disappeared. He left an overnight bag that he didn't come back for and didn't pay his bill. The man had registered as someone else, but from information in his bag, the man's name was Buddy Kraus. According to the clerk, the bag was in the custody of the Oakdale Police Department.

Otis called the motel, saying he wanted to talk with the desk clerk or whoever had registered the man. He then went immediately to the Motel 6 in Oakdale, just a few miles away. He found the clerk, a young Asian college student trying to work his way through school. He hadn't noticed anything unusual about the man, who registered as Buddy Jones. When Otis asked if the man was alone, the clerk said he didn't see anyone else with him. Jones was supposed to stay for two nights, but after the first night he never came back. That sort of thing wasn't too unusual, but when they looked in his overnight bag for a name, they saw it was Buddy Kraus. The clerk had seen the murder announced on the news and knew he should tell somebody about what he had found.

Otis then went immediately to the Oakdale Police Department and they signed the overnight bag over to him as evidence.

Another odd thing was they didn't find a vehicle for Buddy. All the vehicles in the motel parking lot were accounted for, and none was found in the surrounding area. Otis had earlier ordered a check on abandoned or stolen and recovered vehicles to see if anything was found that was registered to Kraus. Not finding a vehicle suggested a second person could be involved.

Back in Deep Lake, Otis itemized the things in Buddy's bag, but didn't find anything unusual. He did a little paperwork and then called Sheriff Walker in Stillwater. He told the sheriff about the trip to Wisconsin and what they had learned about Linda Peterson, particularly. When Otis said he was planning to talk with her that afternoon, Walker said he wanted to be there for the interview. Walker had not expected Otis to find much in Wisconsin and was curious about Kraus's wife and also about the gambling aspect. Convinced as he was of Ethan's guilt, this brought new light to the case and he agreed with Otis that it should be explored. He said he'd head on over to Deep Lake right away.

Otis then called the Deep Lake Bank and asked to speak with Linda Peterson.

She had a quiet soft-spoken voice when she said, "Hello, this is Linda."

Otis decided that beating around the bush wouldn't work and he needed to be blunt and frank with her so he simply explained that he wanted her to come to his office to talk about the death of her former husband, Buddy Kraus.

She took an in-take of breath and was silent for several moments, and then said, "I can be there in fifteen minutes, thank you," and hung up.

Otis pondered her reaction. She offered no denial that Buddy was her husband, and her silence basically gave her acceptance. He wondered what her excuse was to the bank for having to leave.

Sheriff Walker arrived in minutes and Otis suspected he broke the speed limits on Highway 36. Otis got him seated in the conference room, and true to her word, fifteen minutes after his call, Linda pulled up in a plain, tan-colored, five-year-old sedan.

Otis met her at the door and asked if she wanted coffee. She said she didn't, and he led her to the conference room. She was a small woman, dark haired, fortyish, and pleasant looking. She wore pants with a blouse and jacket in earth tones, and appeared quite nondescript, actually like someone who works in a bank, Otis thought.

She was surprised to see the sheriff there, but not overly so. He nodded at her and said simply, "Sheriff Gary Walker."

She replied with her name and sat where Otis indicated.

Both men were sitting across from her, and Otis said, "I've just returned from a trip to Fond du Lac, Wisconsin, where I discovered you were married to Ronald D., known as Buddy Kraus, the man who was murdered recently in St. Paul. Is that true?"

She said softly, "Yes, it's true," and she looked downward.

"Did you kill him?"

She closed her eyes, opened them, then looked Otis in the eye and said, "No, I did not kill Buddy Kraus."

Otis went on, "You know we're going to find out what your situation is anyway. How about you tell us what you know about this killing and anything connected with it. You can start with how you came to be in Deep Lake in the first place. My understanding is that you grew up on the outskirts of Fond du Lac, Wisconsin, and after high school graduation you married Buddy Kraus, a man known to your family and you."

"That's true. I did marry Buddy Kraus, why, I can only guess. My maiden name was Peterson and the Petersons and Krauses have known each other for generations. My mother was friends with Buddy's mother and together they thought I could 'tame Buddy down,' is how they put it.

"He was a selfish person and often hurt others to get what he wanted. He wanted me, and there wasn't much I could do about it. From the beginning I knew I had made a terrible mistake by marrying him. He was possessive, abusive, and just plain mean to me in private. At first, he fawned all over me in public and treated me like a princess, but that didn't last long.

"Unfortunately, I got pregnant. Buddy said it was my fault, and that it was too soon. When Timmy was born with Down syndrome, that was the last straw for Buddy, and he was cruel to both of us both privately and publicly.

"Mr. Jorgensen, it happened that I knew Ethan Thompson's grandmother. She did some speaking on battered wives at my church one time. I talked privately with her and we became friends. When she and her husband moved to Minnesota for his work, I moved there also. With her encouragement, I left Buddy when Timmy was not even three years old. I sneaked away in the night like a criminal so no one would know where I went. She and I stayed close but Ethan never knew about me. I got a job at the bank and am still there. Timmy and I have made friends in the town and I love it here. I hope I never have to leave. I was terrified that Buddy would find me, so I never divorced him. I didn't want paperwork to somehow show my address or any way for him to find me. I'm nervous now, though, about who told you who I am and who from Fond du Lac knows I'm here?"

"That would be the police chief, Chief Sam they call him, and he said he didn't think anyone one else knew."

"Sam Webster. He's a good man, but I didn't tell him where I was going. He's married to Buddy's sister."

"I found that out, too. Let's skip to the night of April seventh. Were you or anyone you know involved in trashing the veterinarian clinic owned by Ethan Thompson?"

"No, absolutely not."

"Tell us about Buddy's gambling."

She let out a sigh. "It was non-stop. Buddy bet on anything and everything. Whenever he had a job with a little money coming in, he used it to gamble on something. He really liked cars—fast racing cars—and he placed bets online if he had money, or with bookies if he didn't."

"Did he support you and Timmy?"

"Not much. I worked in an insurance office for the time we lived in Wisconsin. I was married to him, but I didn't give him any of my money. I have many scars because of that, too, but I needed it to live on. I was determined to support Timmy."

"Tell us more about the bookies. Did you know them? Did Buddy always pay them back?"

"I don't know. I stayed away from him as much as I could for the last couple of years we lived with him. After we left, I never saw him again until the day Buddy came into Joe's and interrupted Ethan's lunch. I was there. I like to have lunch at the restaurant once in a while and watch

Timmy at work. He loves his job at Joe's and he's so thorough about what he does.

"I was sitting nearby when Buddy came in and threatened Ethan. I knew him immediately and was shocked to see him. I heard most of their conversation, but I didn't think Buddy recognized me. My hair used to be lighter and I was very thin. Of course, I knew he would never even look at Timmy and had no clue that the boy with the cart was his son."

"What did you do afterwards? What did you think about seeing Buddy after so many years?"

"I couldn't wait to get out of there. I didn't want him to see me, so shortly after he left the restaurant, I paid my bill and went back to work. I hoped I would never see him again after that. Unfortunately, that didn't happen."

"What did happen?"

"Buddy came to my house when I got home from work. I don't know how he knew where I lived or if he recognized me from the restaurant, but somehow, he found out and showed up there. Another man was with him, a huge man who seemed really rough. Buddy said he was his cousin. Timmy was up in his room with his movie on so he didn't even know they were there."

"So Buddy found you and came to your house. What did he want?"

"Money. Plain and simple. He said he had some debts he had to pay and had lost his house in Wisconsin. He said because I had never divorced him, that meant we were still married and anything that belonged to me, also belonged to him."

"What happened then?"

"He said that I had a cute little house—that's the word he used—cute, but that I needed some updating. I was confused at first, but what he wanted was for me to get a second loan on the house supposedly for re-modeling and give him the money."

"I refused, of course, but that didn't satisfy him. He kept insisting and the other man was goading him on, things like, 'she works in a bank, she can get the money easy,' and kept pushing. Buddy did ask what happened to 'the damn kid,' as he called our son. I told him I was taking care of my boy and he was fine and happy. I think both of them knew Timmy was asleep upstairs and I was afraid he would hear the men and come down, but he didn't. Finally, they both just left. I was terrified they would come back, but I never saw them again."

Sheriff Walker asked, "What did you think when you heard that Buddy had been killed?"

"I was shocked again, but I was glad. I have to say I was glad to hear he was dead and he could never hurt me or Timmy again. But I didn't have anything to do with it. That was the best part. Someone else took care of him for me."

"Tell us about the other man with Buddy. You said he was a cousin. Did you know this man or ever see him before?"

"No. The Krauses have a big family and some people call themselves cousins whether they actually are or not. Most of the Krauses live in what they call Krausville, north of Fond du Lac. Buddy said the man was a cousin, and I didn't ask about him."

"What did he look like, this cousin and did you get his name?"

"I didn't get his name, but he was a big man as all the Krauses are, with a broad face and dark brown hair. He sort of squinted and had brown eyes, I think. He was maybe in his late forties or more, with a beer gut and some wrinkles. He was dressed in jeans and a heavy plaid shirt that looked fuzzy inside so he didn't wear a jacket. He wore a dark-colored cap backwards and his hair stuck out around it, like he needed a haircut."

"That's a good description, thanks. You've given us a lot of information and I'm sure this hasn't been easy for you," Otis said. "Is there anything more we should know about Buddy or the other man, you, or anything connected with Buddy's death?"

"I can't think of anything more right now, but I will let you know if I do. I don't believe that Ethan Thompson is capable of killing anyone. He's always been a gentle man, and a gentleman. But I did see him grab Buddy by his shirtfront and he was angry at that moment. Buddy was going to try to blackmail him, I heard that, and I don't know how Ethan would have reacted later to that threat."

Otis wasn't happy to hear that part, but he thanked Linda for coming in and for her honesty in her relationship with her former husband. She thanked them for listening to her and left to go back to work.

CHAPTER 34
TROUBLE COMPOUNDED IN DEEP LAKE

Sheriff Walker and Otis talked for a while after Linda Peterson left. Otis filled him in on what he had found in Fond du Lac. Walker said, "What a miserable bastard that guy was. I have to say I believe her. You?"

Otis answered, "I do. She had a horrible life living with Kraus. Unfortunately for us, I don't think she killed him. She might have had help, though, and I will be pursuing that. I'm wondering now about the second guy who showed up at Linda's house. What do you think, okay for me to continue searching?"

"You seem really convinced that Thompson didn't do it, even though the physical evidence says otherwise. Considering the questions your trip raised, maybe you should. Yeah, I think there might be more to this than we know. Go for it."

Otis grinned, "I will, and thanks for the confidence."

"It's well earned—you do a good job." As he started to walk out the door, he said, "Find that killer!"

♦♦♦♦♦

McKenzie was enjoying her visit with Mary Jo Jorgensen, and was almost ready to go home with Goldie, when she thought about something. "Mary Jo, what do you know about gambling?"

Mary Jo laughed, "About next to nothing, I'm afraid. Never went in for it 'cuz money's too hard to come by. Why do you want to know?"

"We found out that our murdered guy, Kraus, liked to gamble and we're thinking that's another avenue to travel to find the killer. Know anybody that might know more about it?"

"I know lots of older folks like to go to the Native American casinos and they say they have a great time with the slot machines and poker and things like that. Never been to one myself, so I don't know."

"Older folks, you say?"

"Yeah, the casinos have buses that come to certain places and load up people for day trips to the casinos. I know some retired people from church who love it. They set limits on how much they can lose and have a fun day."

"Hmmm, old guys…thinking about my three old guys who sit downtown and have coffee in the mornings. Haven't seen them for a while and maybe it's time. Thanks Mary Jo—you just gave me an idea. I'll take Goldie home now and maybe Ben and Albert can use the wagon and bring her bowls and toys and stuff when they get home?"

"They will love it, sounds good. It's great to have both you and Otis back home, but it'll be better when you guys can figure how to get Ethan back where he belongs."

McKenzie closed her eyes and frowned; then left with Goldie.

♦♦♦♦♦

The rest of the day flew by after a quick trip to the store for staples, including cookies for Ben and Albert when they delivered Goldies' dishes and toys.

It was late when she was able to sit down and think about what should happen next with her "helping" Otis with the murder investigation. She knew that Otis was going to interview Linda Peterson and wished she could have sat in on that, but she knew he would later share what he found out.

What was really bothering her was the gambling connection. She knew absolutely nothing about gambling, thank God for that, she thought. Her conversation with Mary Jo had her think about exactly who she should approach.

She had made friends the summer before with three older men who usually spent summer afternoons sitting in front of the Ace Hardware downtown Deep Lake. Howard, Fred, and George also had coffee every morning at Joe's, especially on colder days. She had joined them a few times and appreciated their combined knowledge of the town, its businesses, and people.

Through their years these three had worked at a variety of jobs, including the old pickle factory in town, the lumberyard, and one of them in the bank, and they proved to be a priceless source of information, not to mention fun. In fact, it was a suggestion that came from them that helped to solve a murder that she had worked on with Otis the previous fall.

First thing, after her morning run the next day with Goldie, would be to visit the old guys at Joe's. There should be time for coffee before she had to be at work. She could hardly wait.

◆◆◆◆◆

Morning came too soon as McKenzie was out of practice in getting up so early. She did run when she was in New York, but it wasn't nearly the distance or as fun as her run with Goldie through Deep Lake. The two of them took off early and eased into the beauty of it in moments. Both of them grinned through their entire run.

After a shower and dressing for work, she headed to Joe's, hoping her guys would be there. To her satisfaction, they were.

The three older men in their nondescript colorless clothes and caps gave her a slight nod as their way of recognizing her. In their usual understated way of greeting, Fred said, "Wondered if you was ever gonna remember us. George thought you was gettin' too important for us." He nodded at the waitress who immediately brought McKenzie a cup of coffee and topped the others.

"No way that will ever happen. I thought I was considered one of the guys; just can't make it as often as you do. I do have to work, you know."

They shrugged and sipped.

Howard asked, "What's up, girl, you gonna tell us or not?"

Before she could answer, George said, "We know about Doc Thompson being in jail. Looks like a shitty deal to us."

She replied, "To me, too. He's been set up for this killing. Framed by somebody who knew what they were doing. The sheriff and Otis have been working on leads to find out who it was, but they're not getting very far. I hate to say it, but the sheriff thinks Ethan did it. That's how convincing the evidence is. But Otis and I know he didn't. That's what's up, guys, that's the long and the short of it."

They all looked down and sipped in silence a while longer.

"Otis and I went to the town where Ethan and the guy who got murdered used to live. They went to high school together. It's a long story. One thing we learned is that Buddy, that's the murdered guy's name, loved to gamble. Apparently, he bet on anything and everything and always has. Spent anything he could get on it. I'm wondering if you guys can tell me anything about gambling. I have a lot to learn."

"You been under a rock all your life?" Fred asked.

"Not quite, but sometimes it feels like it."

"Some people get it bad—gambling fever they call it," George said. "When they started the Native American casinos in Minnesota and Wisconsin some people went there every day and eventually gambled away everything they had—money, homes, businesses, you name it. They lived on the hope that the next slot machine or crap table was going to be their ticket to riches. It was sad, so sad. Now you can go to places that heal you from the fever and they put out suggestions about betting more money than you have. Some folks still can't stop, but it's better than it used to be. Never had the fever myself and I hope I never do."

The other guys agreed and all shook their heads to indicate they never had it or wanted it, either.

McKenzie offered, "Buddy liked to bet on cars, fast race cars. He went to Road America and racetracks like that where there were opportunities to bet big."

"Whoa, he really did have the fever," Howard said. "That costs money."

"I don't know if he won a lot in the beginning or what, but from our understanding he had money to bet, some of the times anyway."

"How about Milwaukee or Chicago? Did he go there to see races or to bet?"

McKenzie didn't know.

George said, "They do a lot of betting online these days, for horse races, and dogs, and I expect cars, too. But you have to have the money upfront. If this guy knew some bookies and they knew he did come through sometimes, maybe he could get into the bookies for some money on loan."

Fred went on, "If he got too far in and couldn't pay it back, those guys can get nasty. Real nasty, from what I heard."

McKenzie's eyes opened wide. "Do you think that's what might have happened? That Buddy had gambling debts and somebody killed him for that?"

Howard backed off. "We're not saying anything like that happened, mind you, just that it's a possibility. This is a scary world we live in."

McKenzie's mind was whirling. She wanted to talk with Otis, and the discussion with her friends was sounding more and more realistic. It was time for her to get to work anyway, so she left some bills on the table for her coffee and said goodbye.

"You guys seem to always help me get my feet on the ground when I'm having trouble thinking straight. I won't make it so long before next time. Thanks for the lesson and I'll try hard to not ever get the fever."

They all nodded in quiet reply and sipped their coffees.

◆◆◆◆◆

Work. Normally, McKenzie loved her real estate work, but she was so caught up in Ethan's troubles she found it hard to concentrate on what she was supposed to be doing. She needed to find new clients as her friend had taken care of most of her former clients while she was away in New York and had already sold their homes. She did make a bunch of phone calls to leads that came into the office. She also started through lists of former clients and began touching base with them in hopes they could send others her way. Being gone for several weeks didn't help, but she knew she would get back in her personal groove before long.

In the early afternoon, she called Otis and asked if they could talk. He put her off until early the next morning saying he needed to get home for dinner that night. She would stop at the station before going to her office in the morning.

CHAPTER 35
KIDNAPPED IN DEEP LAKE

McKenzie was already at Otis's office before he even got there. She waited for him to open the door and plowed in ahead of him. "What's the deal, you sleep in?" she asked.

He blushed a little, "Well, I've been gone for a couple of nights and we missed each other…the boys have to get ready for school, ya know, and they finally left, and…"

"Oh my God, TMI, TMI, that's enough!" and she grinned.

Otis's phone started ringing and his deputy wasn't there yet. He grabbed it, "Washington…wait a minute there, ma'am, slow down. First, who is this?"

"Linda Peterson. Please help me. They said no police, but you're not really police, and I don't know what to do!"

"Yes, Linda, what's happened? How can I help?" Otis looked at McKenzie and scowled.

"Someone has taken Timmy. He's gone! I've looked everywhere and he's just gone!"

"Your son, Timmy is gone? How do you know he didn't just go to visit a friend, or stop at the store, or something?"

"There was a note left on my kitchen table. I can't believe I slept through something like that. Someone took him and he must have willingly left with them. They had to have tricked him or he would never have left the house without telling me or calling out or something." She started crying then and could hardly speak.

"I'm on my way to your house right now. If the phone rings before I get there, don't answer it. We'll take care of that when I get there. Are you okay with that?"

"Y-yes, please hurry."

"Oboy, Timmy's been abducted. I've gotta call Walker and get over there, right now!"

McKenzie added, "I just looked up her address yesterday, it's 518 Willow. May I follow you? She might need a woman's touch."

"Thanks, and yes!" Otis called Sheriff Walker and when he agreed to go to Linda's house, he took off for her place in his pickup. Linda had said the note said no police, and no one knew if the house was being watched.

When Otis reached Linda's house, she met him at the door with a tear-stained face and was wringing her hands.

"Thank you for coming, Otis. Here is the note I found. I don't understand this at all!"

Otis took the note and it said, "Get $50,000 in 50s and 20s. I will call. The kid is OK. No cops."

"Okay, let's sit down and try to remember everything you can. Tell me when you last saw Timmy." They sat at her kitchen table.

McKenzie came in the door and Otis set her to making some herbal tea to help to calm Linda down.

Between her sobs, Linda was able to tell Otis she had tucked Timmy in the night before at nine, as usual. They had had a quiet evening; she read and he watched videos on his small TV. He was eager to go to his job at Joe's the next day and reminded her that he was the best employee. She smiled and agreed and kissed his cheek, then tiptoed out the door. They both slept with closed doors, and she had gone to bed only an hour later. She read for another hour and went to sleep.

In the morning when Timmy didn't come down for breakfast as he usually did, she went up to wake him. "He wasn't there! I looked everywhere but he was gone. His clothes and shoes were still laid out for morning, so he must still be in his pajamas and slippers. Oh, my poor boy!" she cried.

McKenzie served the tea to Linda and sat with her as Otis called his deputy to bring fingerprinting supplies and meet him at the Peterson house.

When Sheriff Walker got there, having parked his sheriff's car a few blocks away, Otis filled him in on what had happened and he asked, "What makes you think this is an abduction? Maybe Timmy wrote the note himself and maybe he just went to visit a friend or something like that?"

"Timmy is a boy with Down syndrome and his mother knows exactly what to expect from him. He wouldn't go anywhere without asking her permission, or at least telling her where he would be. He's been taken, and I believe the ransom note is exactly that, a ransom note. We need to get someone here who knows how to handle the phone and can record or trace calls."

Walker said, "I'll take care of that right away. I think you might be right."

Otis went on, "My deputy is on his way now and we'll check the entrances especially, for fingerprints, but I doubt if we'll find anything. Gary, I'm leaning toward thinking this has been a professional job all along."

"What do you mean, professional?"

"Buddy Kraus was into gambling in a big way. He knew the world of bookies and risky loans through his connections with the big racetracks. What if he got snared into owing a big amount of money to some important people? People who want their money no matter what?"

"Hell, you think that might be what's happening here?"

"We haven't been able to track Buddy's movements prior to the murder. Nobody seems to have seen him for a while. Do you think he might have been hanging out at one of the racetracks and looking for more money?"

"Well, he wouldn't have been able to get far from the bad guys if that's what happened. They don't forgive easily."

Deputy Lloyd Strother arrived and started looking for fingerprints. Otis helped and the sheriff went back to Stillwater, after saying he would send someone for the phone.

McKenzie was able to keep Linda talking softly as she slightly relaxed from the peppermint tea. Linda believed that whoever took Timmy either made it a game to quietly sneak him out of the house or had somehow threatened him.

She knew it would be extremely frustrating for him if he couldn't get to work at Joe's on time. He could get angry from the frustration and strike out, and this worried Linda because whoever had him may not understand that though Timmy had the fairly strong body of a grown eighteen-year-old, in his mind he was a young boy. She was afraid this could lead to Timmy being hurt or even hurting someone else. She hung her head and gave way to tears.

◆◆◆◆◆

Timmy Peterson was wrapped in a tarp in the back of a pickup truck. He was lying on the floor and felt every bump and turn the vehicle made. Tape covered his mouth and it was hard to breathe with just his nose because that kept running whenever he cried. He was embarrassed and couldn't help crying whenever he thought about what was happening. His eyes were covered loosely but his hands and feet were tied with something and all he could do was roll around in the tarp as he was jolted and joggled in the bed of the truck. Some sort of cover was over the back of the truck because he heard the noise of it after he was pushed into the bottom of the truck.

He was terribly worried about his mom. The man had woken him from a deep sleep and told Timmy his mother was in trouble and needed him to help her. She was somewhere far away and Timmy needed to be very quiet because bad people were in the house.

Timmy did what he was told and quietly tiptoed down the stairs in his pajamas and slippers, even avoiding the creaky step. When he got outside, and had walked a little way, the man hit him—hard—and he fell down. He felt something covering his face and his hands and feet being tied, then being rolled in something stiff and pushed into the back of a vehicle.

The truck started moving and Timmy hoped it was taking him to where he could help his mom. He was scared, but he was more scared for his mom and wanted so much to feel her soft hands on his. Behind the tape on his mouth, he said over and over, "I love you Mom, I love you. Please be safe."

CHAPTER 36
SOMEWHERE IN WISCONSIN

In spite of the rolling and jostling in the truck bed, Timmy finally fell asleep during what seemed to him a long ride. He didn't wake up until the truck stopped for the last time. He had slept through a couple of other stops and wasn't even aware of them.

When he woke up, the man pulled him out of the truck and warned him to not say anything or call out and he would untie him and remove the coverings on his face. Timmy nodded his agreement and was greatly relieved when he could see again, but the pain of the tape ripping off his mouth was more than he could bear, and his tears returned. He was filled with despair with worrying about his mom and the fact that he wasn't able to get to his job at Joe's. He knew they would be looking for him and no one else would be doing his work. How could he be the best employee when he couldn't even be there to do his work?

The man left Timmy's hands tied. He forcefully led him to a shed that had wood piled around it. Timmy looked around and saw a house nearby but the man opened the door to the shed and pushed him in. He also threw in the tarp that had covered Timmy in the truck and told him to sit on a battered wooden chair and to shut up. He said the bad people still had his mother and Timmy needed to be quiet until the man would come back. Timmy did as he was told and was nearly sobbing by this time. The man closed the door and Timmy heard him fiddling with a lock on the other side.

Timmy was alone. Everything was quiet so he sat where he had been told to sit and cried for a long time. After a while he began to look around in the near dark of the room. No windows broke the solid walls, but a little light did seep around the edges of the door he knew was locked, and the ceiling had a few air vents or something between the roof and the walls that allowed some faint light.

His eyes had adjusted to the darkness and he could see piles of junk and boxes around the room and shadows that frightened him. He whispered, "I'm scared Mom, I'm scared. Please find me." He then began to pray the only prayer he knew and hoped that Jesus and the angels would help him and his mom. "Now I lay me down to sleep, I pray the Lord my soul to keep. Thy angels watch me and Mom through the night and keep us safe till morning light. Amen."

Big John Wentworth was indeed a shirttail relative of Buddy Kraus, but he lived near Oshkosh, Wisconsin, farther north than the majority of the family who lived in Krausville. He had connected with Buddy at the big racetrack near Elkhart Lake, and the two became betting buddies.

After dumping Timmy off at the shed, he parked his truck by the house and went in the back entry. His long-suffering wife met him at the door. She looked at the floor with learned obedience and didn't speak until he did.

"Don't go near the shed. There's a homeless guy from the track and I'm keeping him for a while. He's not all there if you get my drift, but he'll need some food now and then. I've got a deal going and I don't want it messed up. Make some grub and I'll take it out now."

Long accustomed to Big John's odd connections and actions, she nodded and started pulling things from the fridge.

◆◆◆◆◆

Big John soon took the food and some water out to Timmy, who woke when he heard the man unlocking the door. He was hungry and the food smelled good, but he also had to go potty and didn't know how to tell the man.

Big John rammed the food tray toward Timmy and untied his hands. He also had a big can that he heaved at him. "This here's your pot. Use that when you have to go. I'll be back tomorrow. *Be quiet!*"

He immediately turned and went out the door before Timmy could say anything, and the sound of the lock was piercing in the surrounding silence. Deeply embarrassed, Timmy used the can and then shoved it as far away as he could. He gratefully gobbled down the tuna fish sandwich and chips and drank the water.

He had nothing more to do so he sat on the chair and quietly said his prayer several times before lying on the tarp and falling asleep, filled with gloom.

CHAPTER 37
BREAKTHROUGH IN DEEP LAKE

Otis sat in his office in complete anguish trying to figure out where Timmy Peterson might be. He had called Chief Sam Webster in Fond du Lac soon after the kidnapping, thinking that whoever had taken Timmy might be connected to the Kraus family. He wasn't yet totally trusting of Sam because of his connection to the Kraus family himself, but he had nowhere else to go.

The phone knocked him out of his reverie. It was Chief Sam and he said he had some news. First, he said, "You're gonna want to get over here right away. I want you to go with me on this one."

Otis jumped up, "I'm already out the door. What's going on?"

"I talked with some more of the Krauses and I really laid a heavy hand on them. Somebody said there was a distant cousin who liked to gamble as much as Buddy, but he didn't live in Krausville. He said the guy moved up near Oshkosh, but he thought the guy gambled with Buddy at the big racetracks sometimes. We even have a name: Big John Wentworth. This could be our break."

"I'm on the way right now. Wait for me." And Otis ran out to his squad car and took off. The lights on the squad car should help him get to Wisconsin a little faster. It was early in the day and he'd call his wife from the car on the way, and also notify Sheriff Walker that he was going to Fond du Lac. He'd pick up Chief Sam and they'd find the guy together.

❖❖❖❖❖

Meanwhile, McKenzie was leaving for work, planning to visit Ethan later that morning. She was already hoping to feel his arms around her and that the rules may have relaxed some. Deep in thought, her phone surprised her. It was Otis's deputy, Lloyd Strother.

"Hello McKenzie. I just had a call from Otis from his squad car. I know you've been helping him with this murder case involving Ethan Thompson. Anyway, Otis said I should let you know that he's on his way to Wisconsin to find Timmy Peterson. You're supposed to rest easy."

"Rest easy, you say? How can I rest easy when I know that Timmy is still in the clutches of a kidnapper?!"

"Well, that's what he said…"

"Do you know where he's headed?"

"Yeah, but I don't know if I'm supposed to tell you."

"You'd better, Deputy, or I'll see that Otis hears that you didn't cooperate with me. You know you don't want that." McKenzie tried to sound as strong and convincing as she could, but she crossed her fingers anyway.

"Well, if you put it that way, I guess it won't hurt for you to know that he's picking up Chief Sam Webster in Fond du Lac, and they're going together somewhere near Oshkosh. The guy they're looking for is called Big John Wentworth."

"Lloyd, I'm leaving now and I'll meet Otis and Chief Sam wherever they're going in Oshkosh. That's closer for me and I don't have to go south to Fond du Lac first. You can tell Otis what I said if he calls in again. Timmy is going to be terrified when he's found and he will need me to take care of him until we can get him home to his mother. Now, get into the police databases that will help you find this Wentworth's address. When you find it, call on my cell because I'll be on my way. Got that?"

"Yes, I do. I'll get on it right away," and he hung up.

"Wow," she thought, "at last we're getting somewhere."

She had filled her car with gas only the night before, so she didn't have that delay, and she took off for Wisconsin.

♦♦♦♦♦

On the way, McKenzie notified her office on her cell phone that she wouldn't be in. Tracey would handle things but told her jokingly she was owed a huge favor. Thank God for friends, she thought. She missed seeing Ethan as she had planned for that day, but if this lead really panned out, she'd be seeing him soon anyway. She breathed a prayer that everything would be all right, then raised her speed control a little higher. As she had hoped, Deputy Lloyd called with Wentworth's address. She promised him she wouldn't confront Wentworth without Otis there, and wouldn't cause trouble. After they hung up, she added quietly, "If I can help it."

♦♦♦♦♦

Timmy had a miserable night and he woke up even more miserable and cold. The man came early when it was still dark with some food and he even dumped the waste can outside and Timmy thanked him. The man just grunted and said again, "Remember to be quiet. I'll be back tonight," and he slammed the door as he left, and of course, didn't forget to lock it.

Timmy eagerly ate the food and wished instead that he had his mother's pancakes. He prayed some more and asked God to send his mother to find him.

♦♦♦♦♦

Big John's wife was curious about the person in the shed. She wondered why he was staying in there and not in the house. She was well conditioned to know of odd things Big John was up to through the years, but this was really strange. He had left early that morning and said he wouldn't be back until late in the day. He again told her to stay away from the shed. She had some laundry to do and decided to hang the clothes on the clotheslines in the back yard instead of using the dryer. They always smelled so good when she did that. Besides, as long as she'd be in the back yard, she might even get a glimpse of the person in the shed without really trying.

An hour later, Sharon Wentworth was indeed using clothespins to hang her just-washed sheets on the line in her back yard. She even hummed a little tune while she worked and had to admit to herself it was pleasant with Big John gone for the whole day.

Timmy suddenly sat up when he heard the woman humming. He thought it sounded like his mother. He went to the door and called out softly at first, "Mom, are you there? Mom, it's me, Timmy. Please let me out, Mom. I don't want to be here!"

As he spoke, Timmy's voice got louder and louder, and Sharon wondered. "That sounds like a child!" she said to herself, "Does he have a child in there?"

She went to the door of the shed and saw that it was locked with a padlock. She said through the door, "I'm not your mom, sonny, but who are you?"

Timmy was greatly relieved and answered, "I'm Timmy Peterson and I'm looking for my mom." He started to cry. "Please let me out, I have to find my mom before they hurt her!"

"What is your mother's name, Timmy, and where do you live?"

Timmy said by rote, "My mom is Linda Peterson. We live at 518 Willow in Deep Lake, Minnesota."

"That's great, Timmy, do you know your mom's phone number?"

Timmy gave the number to her while she tried to open the door. Sharon recognized the lock as a padlock used for miscellaneous things around the house and then remembered where she had seen a key. She ran into her house and searched the kitchen junk drawer to find the extra key.

By the time she returned to the shed, Timmy was sobbing and crying out, "Please let me out, please. I have to find my mom!"

Sharon unlocked the door and Timmy fell into her arms. "Thank you, thank you," he sobbed, "I don't like it in there."

Sharon saw that Timmy was a Down syndrome boy, but he was the size of a full-grown man. She looked at his tear-stained face and his dirty pajamas and slippers and her heart went out to this desolate child.

She led him to the back door of her house saying, "Let's get you cleaned up a little, Timmy, and I'll call your mother to let her know where you are."

♦♦♦♦♦

Sharon tried calling Linda Peterson's home number given to her by Timmy, but there was no answer at around nine-fifteen. There being no answering machine, she just hung up and decided to call later. She worried about what her husband was up to, but expecting she had the whole day before he returned, she concentrated on getting Timmy properly fed and cleaned up. She found some old clothes and even some old leather boots of John's that might fit him well enough and Timmy was delighted.

◆◆◆◆◆

The call to Linda Peterson's house was recorded in Stillwater by the sheriff's department that had tapped her line. They knew the call had come from John Wentworth's home landline, but didn't know, of course, who had placed the call.

The deputy called Otis who was fast approaching Fond du Lac to let him know some action, if minimal, had taken place. Otis was somewhat surprised that Linda wasn't there to answer the call and made him wonder whether she was fully cooperating with the authorities. Otis mulled over his thoughts and kept on his course toward picking up Chief Sam and heading to John Wentworth's house near Oshkosh. The call confirmed even more that Wentworth had Timmy.

CHAPTER 38
ANXIETY IN DEEP LAKE

Linda Peterson was seated on the edge of her chair facing her boss, Don Milligan, at the Deep Lake Bank at exactly nine a.m. She had just explained her need for $50,000 as a home improvement loan and had drawn a small diagram for him what she planned to do with the money to improve her small house. Milligan knew Linda well by her work as an exemplary employee of the bank for many years. He wondered at the amount of the loan, but realized remodeling was expensive and she had plenty of equity in her house to cover the amount she was asking for. However, because of local news he also knew that her former husband had recently been murdered and this seemed like an odd thing to do so soon after that event.

He noted that she didn't seem all that nervous or behaving in a strange way when asking for the loan, so Milligan decided there was no reason he shouldn't grant the loan, and he signed the papers.

Linda seemed relieved when she took hold of the paperwork and went to the window to cash the check. She had already decided to herself that smaller bills would be too risky to ask for and would go with hundreds.

The teller also knew Linda, of course, and was a little surprised when she asked that the check be cashed in total for hundred-dollar bills. Linda told her she wanted to keep track of the money spent and dole it out as needed to the contractors she was hiring to do the work on her house. The teller agreed and put the bills in several large envelopes. After all, it wasn't the oddest thing she had been asked to do in her time at the bank.

Linda told Milligan she had taken the day off to do some administrative cleanup, including arranging for the loan for the remodel. She took her money and left the bank, and no one seemed concerned about her actions.

Back at home, she waited with the burner phone she had been given by the kidnapper. The police didn't know about that phone and no one was monitoring it.

Linda had not told anyone about her visit from the kidnapper when he gave her the phone and instructions for contacting him when she had the ransom amount secured. The big man had returned alone after she had contacted the sheriff's office and they had tapped her home phone. He frightened her enough to do the ransom his way.

She knew he had Timmy from the way he talked, and for some reason, she believed that if she gave him the money, she would get Timmy back. It bothered her to circumvent the police, but he hadn't called as the police expected; he came instead to her home and met with her alone. For whatever reason, she was desperate enough to do what he asked.

After some minutes staring at the phone with fear mounting, she finally dialed the number the kidnapper had given her.

Big John answered on the first ring and said, "I'll be at your house in half an hour. Have the money ready."

Linda sat on her couch and prayed for Timmy's safety.

◆◆◆◆◆

Within thirty minutes John Wentworth skidded to a halt in Linda's driveway and burst into the house, demanding, "Where's the money?"

"Where's Timmy?" she asked anxiously.

"He's safe. I need the money first. Gimme."

She tentatively handed over the envelopes full of hundred-dollar bills.

He looked inside and said, "I told you smaller bills. Whadda you tryin' to do?"

"I was afraid the bank would get suspicious if I asked for small bills. I convinced them that hundreds were okay to use for contractors for the work. Where is Timmy? You said you would bring him home when I got you the money!"

All she got in reply was a grunt. He ran out of the house and jumped in his truck, spinning the wheels in his hurry to get away.

Linda hung her head and sobbed in hopelessness. The money was gone and Timmy was lost to her. She realized what a fool she had been to trust the kidnapper and bypass the sheriff's department.

She thought about McKenzie and how kind she had been to her when Timmy was taken. Maybe she could tell her what she should do now, so she called the number McKenzie had left for her.

McKenzie answered her cell phone. Between sobs and wailing, she finally understood what Linda had done. She was able to calm her a little and told her that Assistant Sheriff Otis Jorgensen knew who the kidnapper was and was on his way to rescue Timmy at that moment.

McKenzie was stretching the truth when she told Linda they knew exactly where Timmy was, but at that point, she believed that was what Linda needed to hear.

"You know where he is?" she cried.

"We do, and we want you to know we'll do everything we can to get Timmy back unharmed. All you can do is wait until you hear from us. Are you okay with that?"

Linda agreed and also said she would call the sheriff's office to tell them what had happened and admit her guilt in contacting the kidnapper without their input.

This was a relief to McKenzie, and she boosted her cruise control one more MPH while praying she would get to Wentworth's home before he did and be able to get Timmy away safely if that's where he really was being held. She also called Otis to let him know what had happened.

"Yeah, Otis here, Kenzie. What's up?"

"I need to let you know I got a call from Linda Peterson. Turns out she had a burner phone from Wentworth for contact and she has already given him the ransom money. He didn't tell her where Timmy is or when or if he'd be released, so she's a real mess."

"Oh shit, that doesn't help things at all! I'm not far from picking up Chief Sam and going to where Wentworth lives. We think Timmy is being held there."

"I should tell you that I'm on the way there, too. I found out from Lloyd where you were headed and I took off not long after you did."

"Whaa, you're going to Oshkosh? Damn it, Kenzie, you're headed for a world of trouble there if what we're suspecting is true. Please stay out of this and let Chief Sam and me handle things—we know how to do it!"

"I'll be careful, you know I will. I'm going to get there just ahead of you and I want to get Timmy away before Wentworth gets back there. I know from Linda that he left Deep Lake before ten-thirty but I'll beat him. I can do this. You know I can!"

McKenzie clicked off her phone and kept driving. Otis shook his head in frustration and turned on both lights and siren to help him go faster. Only God knew how many shortcuts and side roads Wentworth could travel in order to save time.

CHAPTER 39

SHOCK IN OSHKOSH

McKenzie reached Oshkosh in record time and found the address Deputy Lloyd had given her. Being careful as she had promised Otis, she parked a couple of blocks away and walked to the house. She didn't see a pickup anywhere and decided to just knock on the door.

Surprised at the knock, Sharon answered it.

"Mrs. Wentworth?"

"Who are you?"

"My name is McKenzie Ward and I'm here to …"

Timmy heard her voice and came running, "Kenzie!" he shouted, "Sharon is going to find my mom!" and he almost swallowed her with his hug.

Sharon took over, "I think you'd better come in. Timmy obviously knows you and something's going on with my husband and the boy. Timmy has been locked in our shed."

"Yes, something is going on all right. I think it shows that you aren't involved in this, but your husband kidnapped Timmy and has been holding him for ransom. We need to get both of you away from here as soon as we can."

"Kidnapped? Oh, my God, what has John done now?"

"There's more, I'm afraid, but now is not the time to talk about it. You and Timmy must get away from here, now!"

"But John said he'd be gone for the whole day, we should have plenty of time. Let me get a…"

"No, John is on his way right now and he has the ransom money. There's no telling what he will do when he gets here. Come with me now and we'll be safe."

Too late. At that moment, Big John Wentworth came screeching into his driveway and ran into the house.

"Sharon!" he yelled, and then saw McKenzie and Timmy in the kitchen with his wife.

"I should have known—you stupid woman, what have you done!? You let him out, didn't you, you bitch! Who is this?" looking at McKenzie.

McKenzie stood to her tallest height and said with forced confidence, "I'm Timmy's friend and I came to help him. I'm also a friend of Ethan Thompson, the man you and Buddy Kraus tried to swindle in Minnesota. You won't get away with this."

"Like hell I won't. Sharon, are you coming with me? I'm leaving right now!"

"I'm not, John, I've had enough. This time you've gone too far."

Big John took a pistol out of his pocket. "Get over here, kid, you're going for a ride," and he grabbed Timmy.

Timmy stumbled as Big John yanked on his shoulder and he fell into the bigger man, bumping his arm holding the gun. The gun fired wildly, and Sharon screamed as she grabbed her upper leg and fell sideways. She, too, fell into John and bumped his gun hand. The gun fell on the smooth tiled floor. With four pairs of eyes watching the shiny pistol slide away as if in slow motion, Timmy picked up his foot clad in John's old leather boot and kicked it far away.

As they all took a frantic breath, the door burst open and Otis and Chief Sam surged in with guns drawn.

John appeared anything but big as he folded in on himself in sudden realization of all he had done. Sharon was crying softly as she lay bleeding on a throw rug she had braided years before, and McKenzie held Timmy in her arms, both of them wide-eyed and panting with fear and relief.

CHAPTER 40
TROUBLE RESOLVED IN DEEP LAKE

McKenzie sat on her living room sofa curled in the embrace of her love. Ethan Thompson was pale, thin, and shaggy-haired, but his eyes were bright and remained locked on McKenzie as if she were his last meal.

Otis and Mary Jo sat in easy chairs across from them, while Ben and Albert played happily in the basement with Isabella and both of the dogs, Honey and Goldie.

The scene was as beautifully domestic as anything could possibly be, however their conversation was anything but.

Two days earlier, as soon as John Wentworth was in custody of Police Chief Sam Webster and held in the Fond du Lac jail awaiting arraignment, Otis had called Sheriff Walker in Stillwater and asked that Ethan be released straight away.

McKenzie left Wisconsin immediately to be there to meet Ethan as he left the Washington County Jail. Several hours later, their reunion was better than a romance novel as they hugged each other in the jail's parking lot while smiling, kissing, laughing, crying, and just holding each other for what could appear to be an attempt to break a Guinness World Record for embracing.

After John's apprehension, Otis headed back to Deep Lake with Timmy and the ransom money for a joyful reunion with his mother. Many tears were shed, as would be expected. Timmy could hardly wait to get back to work at Joe's, and was excited to tell his story to anyone who would listen.

Otis returned to Fond du Lac, by plane this time, to deal with final details and evidence surrounding the epic saga of Buddy Kraus and John Wentworth's crime spree.

◆◆◆◆◆

That evening Otis told them the results of all that had transpired.

"John Wentworth opened up and spilled it all after he was dragged out of his house by Chief Sam. He had killed a man who was his friend with no remorse whatsoever, but shooting his wife by accident seemed to just do him in. He watched her bleeding on the floor and caved. He knew it was all over."

Mary Jo interjected and wrung her hands, "It's hard for me to even think that people like that are out there. What causes someone to do such terrible things?"

Otis answered, "Greed, my dear, for money and power. The pressure was building from past actions and Buddy knew he was in trouble. As we found out early on, Buddy Kraus was a heavy gambler. We learned from his wife, Linda, that before she left him, he spent nearly everything they had on gambling of some kind. His favorite racket was to bet on the fast-car races at the big tracks. Any time he could get a stake together he would leave for the racetracks. It was there he ran into his distant cousin, John Wentworth. Between the two of them they managed to hang out together often and place their bets. Sometimes they won, with a lot of celebration, but they invariably managed to lose again down the line. They were always searching for money. They knew the bookmakers who would sometimes give them credit, but Buddy got in deeper with them than John did.

Buddy needed money badly because he knew the bookmakers had "friends" who liked to give pain in place of unpaid debts. He remembered Ethan from school, and he and John decided Ethan might be a good source to use Buddy's blackmail ploy.

Here Ethan broke in, "Even I didn't know that the statute of limitations had run out long ago for the fire in the country. I guess I'm not any smarter than they were." He hung his head and McKenzie realized then that Ethan had suffered badly from his experience in jail, and it was going to take time for him to gain back his self-respect and confidence. She shared a glance with Otis and knew he understood.

Otis said, "To be frank here, that's not something the average Joe thinks about. You're not a lawyer, you know.

"Yeah," Ethan mumbled, and McKenzie leaned in even closer and stroked his arm.

"Let me go on with the story—it gets complicated," Otis continued. "After a bit of alcoholic courage-building, Buddy and John went together to Deep Lake to threaten Ethan Thompson, but they stayed in different cheap motels just to be safe. That was a good move on their part, and it kept us from finding out about John for quite a while.

"They cruised the town and Buddy told John about seeing his wife in the restaurant when he had confronted Ethan. He did some searching on his phone and found where Linda lived. He saw she had returned to her maiden name and they had some discussion about that. They also found where Ethan's clinic was.

Otis continued, "Buddy paid a visit to Linda first, and scared her pretty bad but left with no plans made about how to get any money from her. Then Buddy and John just wanted a little 'fun' and decided they'd put the fear of God into Ethan by ransacking his clinic. That night they used a couple of baseball bats from the back of John's truck, smashing and destroying everything in sight in the clinic. During the free-for-all, John found the syringes and heavy meds and pocketed them for himself. At some time while he was alone, he must have studied the syringes to know which ones were the most lethal.

"After the fracas the two of them went for an early breakfast at an all-night diner and laughed themselves silly over how much fun it had been to destroy a man's life's work."

Everyone in the room just shook their heads at this sad statement.

"The men had been talking about how they were going to hit Ethan with the blackmail scam and also figure out a way to get some money from Linda, now that Buddy had found her. After all, she had never divorced Buddy that he knew of, and as her legal husband he was part owner of her house. I think that's where John got the idea of dumping Buddy and getting some money out of Linda for himself.

"After breakfast, they headed toward their motels, but stopped on the way in a shadowy alley in St. Paul for John to take a whiz. Buddy got out, too, and John hit him over the head with one of the ball bats. Buddy must have fallen to the ground and that's when John pulled out the syringe and strongest sedative and injected a large amount of the drug in Buddy's arm.

"He wore gloves so the only fingerprints found were Ethan's, made as he had arranged the items in his cabinet at the clinic.

"After that, John checked out of his motel, went back home and waited a few days. Then he figured out a way for Linda to apply for a home mortgage and get some cash for supposed repairs and remodeling, as he and Buddy had talked about. He decided to take Timmy and hold him for a while to be sure she would pay up. John took Timmy in the night and stashed him at his home in Wisconsin, keeping him in a shed in the back yard.

"As you know, Linda called me as soon as she realized Timmy was gone, and we arranged for phone tapping and having someone at the office listen to see if the kidnapper would call.

"What we didn't know was that John went back to Linda and gave her a burner phone to use in contacting him and scared her enough to keep her from calling anyone from the sheriff's office, including me. We hadn't expected that, I have to say."

Ethan said, "I don't know how anyone can think of everything. I'm blown away by this whole thing and how people can think up ways to hurt others and even kill them to steal what they've honestly earned and built up." He shook his head and tightened his hold on McKenzie.

"You're right," Otis answered, "and that's what makes my job so necessary in this crazy world. We caught this one, thank God. With the help and cooperation of Chief Sam Webster in Fond du Lac, and some perseverance and dogged belief in your innocence, Ethan. McKenzie bugged everybody involved and even put herself in danger to catch John Wentworth."

"I think we're a mutual admiration society here, Otis," McKenzie said. "And we're both really thankful for Chief Sam because he was instrumental in pinpointing Wentworth."

Otis answered, "You got that right, Kenzie. Now it looks like we've all got a big job in helping Ethan get his clinic rebuilt. Besides helping our friend, it's time for all of us to get back to the day jobs we're getting paid for! To be honest, I wouldn't mind just handing out parking tickets for a while." The laughter that followed relaxed all of them.

Ethan finally stood and raised his glass to Otis and McKenzie, saying, "I second that motion, Otis. Thank God for both of you and your faithful belief in me or I might have rotted away in that horrible jail. Instead, we're all here together and life can go on. Next week is Easter, and I mean to be ready to take care of pink bunnies and little green chicks and ducks. Bring 'em on, Deep Lake!"

ABOUT THE AUTHOR

Trouble in Deep Lake is the third novel in the award-winning Deep Lake series, following *Danger in Deep Lake*, and *Death in Deep Lake*, cozy mysteries set in a small town in rural Minnesota, not far from the metropolis of the state's Twin Cities. Gloria VanDemmeltraadt, writing as Gloria Van, wrote the fictional series.

Other books: Gloria VanDemmeltraadt's first book, *Musing and Munching*, is both a memoir and a cookbook.

Much of her work focuses on drawing out precious memories. As a hospice volunteer, she continues to hone her gift for capturing life stories and has documented the lives of dozens of patients. She refined this gift in *Memories of Lake Elmo*, a collection of remembrances telling the evolving story of a charming village. She continues her passion and has caught the essence of her husband's early life in war-torn Indonesia. In *Darkness in Paradise*, Onno VanDemmeltraadt's story is touchingly told amid the horrors of WWII. This work has been praised by Tom Brokaw and has also earned the New Apple Award for Excellence in Independent Publishing for 2017 as the Solo Medalist for Historical Nonfiction.

The theme of legacy writing continues with a nonfiction booklet, a clear and concise how-to manual called *Capturing Your Story: Writing a Memoir Step by Step*.

Gloria lives and writes in mid-Minnesota. Contact her through her website: gloriavan.com.